WHO
LOST,
I FOUND

— *stories* —

Broken Eye Books is an independent press, here to bring you the odd, strange, and offbeat side of speculative fiction. Our stories tend to blend genres, highlighting the weird and blurring its boundaries with horror, sci-fi, and fantasy.

Support weird. Support indie.

brokeneyebooks.com
twitter.com/brokeneyebooks
facebook.com/brokeneyebooks
instagram.com/brokeneyebooks

WHO LOST, I FOUND: STORIES

"Eden Royce is among the most vital and vibrant voices working in the horror and fantasy genres today. Now with her latest collection, *Who Lost, I Found: Stories*, she once again delves into the haunted lives of women and girls in ways that are by turns surprising, heartbreaking, horrifying, and utterly empowering. Needless to say, every tale in this table of contents is a knockout. Read this incredible book, and then be sure to recommend it to all your friends." (**Gwendolyn Kiste**, Bram Stoker Award-winning author of *The Rust Maidens, Pretty Marys All in a Row*, and *Reluctant Immortals*)

"In *Who Lost, I Found*, Eden Royce treats readers to a Southern Gothic literary feast. Prose that sings and stories that pluck on all the right heartstrings. This collection is a beautifully nuanced blend of Gothic horror and folklore, the kind of tales that will linger long after you've read the last line." (**Veronica G. Henry**, author of *Bacchanal, The Quarter Storm*, and *The Foreign Exchange*)

"Endlessly absorbing. A charismatic, ensnaring collection of haunted locales and legacies, with a magic both bloody and wondrous. I couldn't tear myself away. Royce deftly navigates her sea of stories to enchant your imagination, make your skin crawl, and even break your heart." (**Hailey Piper**, Bram Stoker Award-winning author of *Queen of Teeth*)

"In *Who Lost, I Found*, Eden Royce's lyrical prose invites readers into the lives of Southern conjure women, haints, sentient houses, Mami Watas, and caterers of the dead. A house gets up and moves inland when it senses a hurricane brewing. A death row inmate makes an unusual request for her last meal from a BBQ joint that offers more than meets the eye. A graverobbing rootworker uses tea magic to bring home the lost bodies of lynching victims. A djinn braids hair and changes lives at a salon. And a weaver guards the veil between worlds. Skirting the lines between the surreal, horror, and fantasy, *Who Lost, I Found* is a triumph of a collection by a supremely gifted writer that deserves nothing but the highest praise." (**Yvette Lisa Ndlovu**, author of *Drinking from Graveyard Wells*)

WHO LOST, I FOUND

- stories -

Eden Royce

WHO LOST, I FOUND: STORIES
by EDEN ROYCE

Published by
Broken Eye Books
www.brokeneyebooks.com

All rights reserved.
Copyright © 2023 Broken Eye Books and the author.
Cover illustration by Marcela Bolívar.
Cover and interior design and editing by Scott Gable.

978-1-940372-68-6 (trade paperback)
978-1-940372-69-3 (hardcover)

Table of Contents

Every Good-Bye Ain't Gone

MIXIE SMELLED CHICKEN PURLOO COOKING WHEN SHE GOT HOME from work and knew someone had died. In her thirty years, the only time her mother ever cooked was when a person had passed on and someone needed to speak with the dead.

She strode over to the pot bubbling away on the stove and lifted the lid. The fragrance of smoked pork rolled out, along with the scent of roasting chicken broth, and fresh thyme from the back garden. She stirred it to inhale more of the essence, but she knew better than to eat mama's magic.

Instead, she strolled to the fridge and stared at the offerings inside. "Who died?" she asked.

Her mother was chopping away at something on a cutting board, her back to Mixie, the knife crunching wetly through.

"None of your business."

"Yeah, but who?" Mixie found a peach, almost too soft; she could feel the pit loosening inside its housing of flesh. She took it to the sink to rinse off the downy coating of fuzz.

When she was younger, she'd been too eager to eat the fruit and regretted the itch the fuzz left. Rubbing made it worse, the inside corners of her mouth taking the brunt of the friction. It was like the make-out session she'd had with Silvio that one time. Her lips had felt over-soft, bruised, and she couldn't stop touching them. Pushing the thought away, she turned on the tap full blast and shoved the fruit under.

Mama turned to look at Mixie, her hair in two braids tight to her scalp. Sucked her teeth. "Who do you think?"

She wracked her brain trying to think of whose favorite meal was purloo. Charlestonians loved rice, but most of those Mixie knew preferred other dishes: rich red rice or jambalaya or even cold rice pudding—a sausage made from pork and herbs. Who loved purloo enough to come back to this side for it?

"I don't know." Mixie picked at the peach skin with a fingernail until it loosened, then peeled it away in strips. Dangled each over her mouth before dropping it in. Then she realized. "Oh . . ."

She hadn't thought of Terrell in so long, she'd forgotten his favorite food. But why? Who was bringing back her ex-husband?

Every good-bye ain't gone. Words she'd been hearing her whole life. The family had turned it into a motto. Better than Caterers for the Dead, she supposed. The Upshaws cooked food for the deceased, and combined with the right people, the right timing, the right prayer, their spirits would return to answer questions, give advice, tell truths.

"Before you ask, his wife requested a full service. Chose the most expensive plan we offer." Mama's knife flew through an onion, dicing it into small chunks. She dropped them into a large stewpot with a smoked pork neck bone and turned on the burner. "And you know we need a real good reason to turn down that kinda money."

A full service meant that woman—what was her name? Neicy? Neely?— wanted all three: questions, advice, and truths. So they would have to make three dishes. The chicken and rice was cooking, and a pile of washed collard greens waited in the sink. Mixie put down her peach to gather the greens, her movements wooden. She pushed the leaves into the sizzling pot, then covered them with water from the teakettle on the stove, followed by the lid.

Why now? Terrell's been dead almost a year. We were divorced for six months before that. And he'd been with that woman—was it Nancy?—a year or so before we split up. That I know of.

When Mixie looked up, mama was watching her. Close. Like she already knew the litany playing in her daughter's mind. "You don't have to go tonight, you know. I can get your brother—"

"I'm better at communicating than he is." Except, it seemed, when it came to Terrell.

"I know." Mama wiped her hands on a dishcloth.

"So?" Mixie asked, wondering if her mother was going to make two sacrifices tonight. First the chicken, second making her stay home and using her brother as focus for the sitting instead. Benjamin was a great cop, but he didn't have Mixie's experience with the dead.

"So I guess you're going. Get me the butter. I need to make a pie."

She pulled the fridge door open again and took out the box of waxed-paper-wrapped sticks. "Pecan?"

Mama's face froze. Then a little frown formed between her eyebrows. "No . . . sweet potato."

Since when? Terrell's favorite dessert was pecan pie. No ice cream, no whipped cream. Just plenty of bourbon and sugar in a crisp, flaky crust that shattered when touched with a fork. Nuts chopped instead of whole.

"Oh, right," Mixie said. "Want me to make it?"

"No, you get washed up and changed. I put everything in the boxes already. We need to be there at seven."

Mixie glanced at her phone. She had three hours to get her head right for the sitting. Spirits could tell when something was off. Sometimes they'd ignore your efforts. Other times, they'd make a beeline for that flawed spot inside of you. The one that's worn away, leaving a tiny hole that never gets filled no matter how happy you are. And that, Mixie knew, was so much worse.

"I need a bath."

Mama nodded. "Good idea. Take as long as you need," she called out as Mixie walked away to the bathroom. "Refill the tub, if you have to."

Mixie sprinkled the water in the tub with bluing and climbed in. The claw foot stood in the middle of the room, still in its pride of place since the house was built during Reconstruction after the Civil War. Mixie's family had been cooking for the dead since before Juneteenth, when the slaves were finally freed. Her family had been lucky to get the land for the price they had, even luckier to avoid the ire of those who detested the nineteenth of June.

She reclined in the steaming water, laced with salt for purity and rosemary for clarity of mind, and let her thoughts drift. Had Terrell forgotten he liked pecan pie? Maybe that woman he married didn't know how to make them right. He'd lost a great deal of weight when she'd seen him last to ask about the house. Sure, what's her name lived there, but part of that down payment had been hers. Wasn't she owed something?

Absently, she lathered a cloth with castile soap and washed thoroughly. Sweet potato pie. Mixie doubted that woman knew how to make a decent one. You had to boil the sweet potatoes in their skins to keep out the water, or it would drain away their flavor. Then peel the tough skin away and put the orange flesh through a ricer to remove the fibrous parts.

There was no reason to care, was there?

They'd split up, Mixie leaving the house she'd shared with Terrell and coming back to her mother's after the divorce. That woman moving in.

It was over because he hadn't come first.

I'm what, Mixie? Third on your list of priorities?

He'd been fourth actually, after God, and mama, and cooking.

And this magic . . . he'd scoffed, waved his hand like he was clearing a room of a foul smell. Like her magic was nothing—a silly fancy not real enough to acknowledge with words. Like she wasn't enough. But no one can separate a witch from her magic, unless she wants to be. Even then, it would wind its way back, bringing a good reason to take up the candles and the herbs and the whispers again.

You're a teacake, Mixie. Like those desserts you make. He'd avoided calling her chocolate . . . small mercy. A fancy sweet that melts away. I need a meat and potatoes woman.

And he got one. Mixie had her ears out there and she'd heard Terrell's new wife was no filler, no fluff. Work, eat, sleep, work again. Presumably, fuck was somewhere in that list because Terrell did like all his hungers satisfied. She kept his clothes looking good too: fresh from the cleaners, immaculate, creases sharp, and in them, he marched around like a peacock.

A few weeks after they split, Mixie dreamed of fish, and she knew the woman was pregnant. But these fish weren't the usual docile schools of bubbling swimmers. They were hideous, hunchbacked sea monsters, their twisted maws full of needle-like teeth. Mama sent a baby shower gift, even though Mixie asked her not to. A lavender baby blanket, kitten soft, with a tiny, stitched moon yawning among a scattering of stars.

She bore no ill will toward Terrell; they'd wanted different things out of life. But on some nights when the air carried a chill, she had a fleeting moment of missing him. And she wondered how happy he was. Would she take him back? No, never. Well . . . probably not. But she wouldn't get the chance to dwell on the decision.

Soon, Terrell was dead, and no one knew what happened to the baby, if indeed there had been one. His burial was quick after the postmortem, which found arteries clogged like a man's twice his age. Natural causes, the coroner said. No foul play. Just a heart attack while driving and a subsequent drowning in the Ashley River. Mama had gone to the funeral. She'd come home from the cemetery and the repast, complimenting the beautiful service and berating the choice of caterer.

"Cake squares. Can you believe it? I'll bet they were from a mix," she'd chortled. "It should have been petits fours. You serve delicate cakes for the bereaved. Doesn't anyone know that?"

Mixie had agreed, not looking up from her book, making sympathetic noises as her mother prattled on while changing out of her Sunday best.

A timer went off in the kitchen, jolting Mixie out of her reverie. She sat up, poured a cup of the salt and rosemary bathwater over her head three times, then climbed out. Said a prayer before pulling the plug. Mixie anointed her curls with Crown of Success oil and let the excess drip onto her body, where it left shimmering trails before she smoothed the rivulets into her skin.

What could that woman want from Terrell now? Questions, advice, and truths?

Maybe, Mixie thought, pulling a white cotton dress over her head, just maybe she could get some questions of her own answered.

Mixie walked behind her mother up the stairs to the porch of the woman's house. She carried the family's signature cake boxes with the requested sweet potato pies, deep sienna with teal script. Her mother carried the empty chafing dishes, tins of fuel gel, and boxes of candles with extra-long fireplace matches.

Her brother Benjamin, beast of burden that he was, was heavy laden with dishes of hot food.

When the door opened, Mixie's shoulders tightened. But the woman removed the pinched look of disapproval from her heavily contoured face quickly enough. Her wig was made of human hair, Mixie noted, but it wasn't a style that flattered her.

"Appreciate you for coming," she said. The door swung wide.

"Thank you kindly, Nathalie," Mama said, and Mixie rolled her eyes. "Come on," she hissed when her daughter hesitated before stepping inside.

The house was air conditioner cold; none of the sweet heat of the outside breeze penetrated these walls. When she had lived in this house, Mixie had kept the windows cracked open during the day to allow fresh air to blow through, taking with it stale, stagnant scents.

Mixie, her mother, and her brother followed Nathalie to the dining room where five chairs surrounded a table laid with five place settings.

"Over there." Nathalie pointed to the table and folded her arms across her chest to watch while the Upshaws arranged the mise en place for the sitting.

Thick white linen cloth draped the mahogany table. A taper candle, unscented as to not disturb the aroma of the food, went into each of the house's three silver candelabras.

"Good thing I don't have to use mine," mama whispered. "And you smell like cinnamon. You're not trying to get that man back, are you?"

"He's dead, Mama."

"So what?" she asked while Benjamin set down the trays of hot food and placed them in the chafing dishes. Both women watched as he popped the tops off cans of fuel gel and placed them under the dishes. Finished, he stepped back to his mother and sister.

Mama lit the fuel, then nodded to her daughter.

"We ask for guidance and safe passage," Mixie intoned, her voice clear and silvery. "Blessings for this food the dead are about to receive. May it nourish their souls with memory and feed our bodies with their words."

"Touch and agree," her mother said, taking Mixie's right hand.

"Touch and agree," Benjamin parroted, slipping one of his slender, rough hands into each of the women's, completing the circle.

Power arced between their joined hands, the jolt feeling like a knife slipped through tender skin. First, only pressure. Then, the sting, sharp and hot, followed by a throb of pain that pulsed in time with Mixie's heartbeat. An aching, lazy pulse, thick and slow as spun honey. Her mother rode it out, face not changing expression, but Mixie saw the control she used to pull off that feat.

Benjamin's face was the picture of awe, head tilted back to look at the ceiling as if it was the first time he'd ever seen a sunset over the ocean. Mixie smiled through her own pain. He really hadn't had the chance to experience much of the family magic. Full services were rare, as they typically held sittings consisting of one dish that could be accomplished with two people. She squeezed his hand, and he looked down, then across at her, bestowing his radiant smile.

"We're ready," mama said, gesturing for everyone to take a seat.

They unwrapped the food, and steam rose in misty whorls, bringing the scents of Terrell's favorites: roasted, herb-laden chicken, the rice it lay on having soaked up the cooking liquor until it was plump and soft, and the collard greens, wilted from their shared bath with smoky pork, sprinkled with a spicy vinegar to cut through any lingering richness. Heady scents made Mixie's stomach rumble. Mama opened one of the two boxes of pie.

Nathalie's mouth was in a hard line. Her table was set with beautiful china. Mikasa, unless Mixie missed her guess, and her silverware was polished to a mirror quality. Stone-faced, she said, "I can ask now?"

"Just a minute," Mama said with kindness, but Mixie wasn't fooled. She knew mama had seen the woman's reaction to their ritual, this feeding of the dead, and had deemed it beneath her. Even so, mama dished up the food onto the warmed plates and passed them out to everyone. Terrell got his own serving. "This is a nice meal, and we're all going to act like we're enjoying it."

"Thanks for cooking, Ma," Benjamin said.

"Smells good, Mama."

"You're both welcome."

Nathalie watched while they shared around the food, talking as though it were a normal Sunday dinner. Finally, she took her fork and began to push the food around on her plate. So her thanks weren't forthcoming.

Mixie looked at her mother who shrugged. She'd never seen someone as unwilling to participate when they'd specifically asked for their services. She hoped her mother asked for payment up front.

Now was as good a time as any. Mixie struck one of the fireplace matches and lit each taper candle. The flames flared up halfway to the vaulted ceiling before settling to a gentle glow.

"Call him," mama whispered to Nathalie. When the woman shook her head, mama frowned. "You still want this? Then you call your husband to the dinner table."

"Terrell? Honey . . . dinner." Nathalie's whispered croak wouldn't have brought a rabbit to carrots.

"He's dead, not in the next room."

"Mixie," mama scolded.

The woman cleared her throat and tried again, not managing to do much better. Mixie had enough.

"Terrell! Ter-rell James Hamilton, time for dinner!" The words felt familiar in her mouth—chewy sweet, tangy on the back of her tongue—and she winced at how good they tasted.

The candle flames shuddered and flared again, illuminating the faces of those around the table. When the flames returned to normal, they saw a three-fingered pinch missing from one of the pies.

Nathalie gasped, her fork clanging to her plate. She brought her hands to her mouth, pressing in her scream, Mixie guessed. But Mixie wasn't surprised. Terrell had always stolen a bit of dessert before dinner. He loved to say, Never know if I'm gonna make it to dinner, do I?

As they watched, the skin and flesh melted from a chicken thigh resting at the edge of the plate between Mixie's and Nathalie's, pinched away to nothing. Nathalie scooted her chair back, but mama stopped her from rising from her seat with a glare. The leaves of tender collards formed into pyramids, as if picked up in eager fingers, and wafted into nothingness. The air conditioner stuttered to a stop, but the heavy chill lingered. For some reason, it didn't affect the heat of the food.

When Terrell's plate was empty, a shadow darted between the chafing dishes on the table. Mixie heard Nathalie's tremulous warbling and cut her eyes at the woman. She'd asked for this. Mama had explained everything and prepared her. But she obviously hadn't listened. Or understood. Not really.

Like so many people, Nathalie heard what she wanted and filtered out the rest. Mixie envied people who were able to do that. She heard the voices of the dead so often, it had become like she was sitting at a family meal all the time.

The shadow lingered over the hot food, hovered like a thick stream of coiling smoke off a charcoal grill or the acrid plumes of a burnt-to-a-cinder dish. Sniffing. Sampling. A raw, snuffling sound, of wild and hungry animals clawing for a meal.

Mixie's arm throbbed. She looked down, expecting to see a cut, a flesh one, but there was nothing marring her brown skin. A vein twitched. Terrell had eaten of each dish, and any minute, mama woul—

"Ask now," mama said.

But Nathalie was staring. Staring at the void of inky mist that used to be her husband, whose tendrils now sank into the steaming rice, picking. Devouring. Her plump lower lip trembled, jiggled jelly-like.

The candles flickered, flame and smoke consuming the molded soy wax. Mixie sat back, sipped her wine. If Nah-tha-lee didn't hurry up, all the food would be gone and along with it her opportunity to know whatever it was she needed to.

"What's your question?" mama prompted. "Quickly."

The shadow didn't seem to notice the trauma going on at the table. It continued to consume, making snuffling sounds, a pig after a truffle. The darkness of its form grew, deepened into a richer, more solid black. The tendrils' reach grew as well. Now they almost touched the walls.

"Damn," Mixie said. "Did you not feed him?"

Nathalie's head snapped toward Mixie, and her upper lip curled. "He ate too much junk! That was your doing."

"Mine?"

She thumped her well-manicured hands down on the table. "Yes, yours! He was used to that rich, salty food you cook. What was I supposed to do? Say, 'Terrell, will you please eat more vegetables?'"

Nooooo . . .

The answer stretched through the room, cavernous and resonant, ending on a sizzling hiss. Nathalie's sneer dropped, face slackening with shock. She stiffened, her nails scraping along the linen tablecloth as she clenched her hand into a fist.

"That wasn't my question, and you know it." Her words were ground out, powder fine. "You—"

"Careful, you only have advice and truth left." Mixie pursed her lips. "Better not waste them."

"Girls!" mama said, a frown marring her unlined brown forehead. "Yes, I called you grown-ass women girls 'cause that's how you're acting. This is a sitting, not a playground."

Mama continued, ignoring their pouts. "Go on now and ask for your advice. Hurry, we don't have a lot of time."

A deep pull of breath in, released on a bourbon-soaked puff. "Terrell, how can I sell this house? I don't have the deed, and the cost of upkeep is breaking me."

Mama's eyes flicked to Mixie, and she shrugged.

The shadow stilled in its consumption. Its tendrils contracted, pulled closer to the main splot of dimness, solidifying. A face—possibly Terrell's—formed in the amoeba-like matter then dissolved before reforming into something haphazard, confused, thrown together without thought. The neck, though, was evident. Well-defined. It stretched, pulled taut, as if the shadow reached for something with its jumbled muddle of a head. Lumps, like those in a fed snake's belly, moved thickly, painfully down its corded gorge on a choked swallow.

Then breakkk . . .

Huffs of stale air made Mixie realize the shadow was laughing.

Breakkk like you broke me . . .

Fear crawled along Nathalie's face, and Mixie could see the stain of heat rising up her neck even in the dim room. She pressed her smile into the rim of her wineglass. How could she have missed this?

Nathalie wasn't amused. "This is some kind of joke. You're . . . you're all playing with me, aren't you? It's sick. What you're doing. Sick."

The fine tremors in her body made the encroaching tendrils wispy and fine. They retracted, a pulse of vapor, then advanced again, coiled around the legs of Nathalie's chair.

"No, child. We haven't done anything sick." Mama's face was impassive, her voice clear but soft. "Have you?"

"How dare you," Nathalie growled. She threw her wine in mama's face. Droplets splashed on one of the candles, extinguishing it and leaving the tang of vinegar in the air.

The entire room waited a breath.

In. Out.

"You must be looking to die," Benjamin said.

Nathalie's hand closed around her table knife. "Try me." She bolted up from her chair, scraping it back. Before the knife cleared the table, the tendrils tugged, and the chair shot forward again, knocking the woman's legs from under her. Her ass hit the seat, then her chest crashed against the table. Air whooshed from her lungs, endangering the life of another candle.

"Hmm." Mama touched her strand of pearls. "You might want to come clean about it, whatever it is."

"What are you doing to me?"

The tendrils pulled the chair forward again. Mixie thought she could hear a crunching, a crushing. All that tooth grinding Nat was doing set her own teeth on edge. Mixie unzipped her purse, fished around, finally coming up with a piece of gum. Popped it in her mouth and chewed, glad for the minty buffer.

"We're not doing anything. All we do is lure the spirit back. How they act toward you . . . varies." Mama narrowed her eyes. "Ask for your truth. While you have breath."

"Let me go!"

Benjamin looked up from his place setting where he was folding his napkin into a bow tie. "That's not really a question."

"Aren't you going to help me?" Her voice wheedled out, nails clawing, scratching at the linen. Mixie looked at her mother.

"We can stop this now if you release us from the full contract. We'll retain all payment, of course. All I have to do is extinguish the candles." Mixie eyed her. "But you won't get your truth, Nat."

Chair legs scraped again.

"No." Nathalie dragged in a breath—Mixie wasn't sure how, with that table digging into her torso, but she managed it—and coughed it out. "Terrell, tell me where the deed is. The truth."

Terrell's shadow rose to hover above the table. It pulled itself forward by those tendrils until it was nose to inky, amorphous matter with Nathalie.

You firrrrrst . . . Truuuth . . .

The shadow grasped her upper arms, shook her, or maybe Nat was shuddering so hard her teeth rattled. Mixie bit down on her molars, the gum between them popping like bubble wrap. The candle stuttered. Not much longer now.

"How—" mama began.

"Ha! I knew sweet potato wasn't his favorite."

Mama's mouth twisted, and Mixie knew she was going to get an earful in the car. But her words were for Nathalie. "Answer him, child!"

The chair eased back, enough to allow her to drag in a breath. Her eyes darted around the table, but she didn't get a response from any of the Upshaws or from Terrell. She sighed, coughed. A drop of blood reddened the white linen.

"Oh, I'm tired of this." Mixie pushed her chair back, stood. "I used to live here, so I know the places to hide things."

Mama's mouth opened, like she was about to tell her daughter's head a mess. But she thought better of it and closed her mouth again as Mixie stomped off and out of the room.

As large as the house was, Mixie moved through it with speed. Each step felt more familiar, despite the woman's ill-advised changes in décor. She looked in the cabinet under the kitchen sink to find half-used bottles of her favored cleaners. Behind the loosened tile in the master bathroom, she discovered a roll of what looked like mold-softened bills. She shook her head and replaced the square of porcelain, leaving its secret intact.

In the garage, she swung open the door to a small closet, revealing Terrell's suits and casual clothes. From them, the eye-watering scent of chemicals wept out. It was overwhelming, as if this door hadn't been opened since his death. Mixie staggered under the reek of it, tasting sharp and metallic as it choked her. Stumbling, she steadied herself on a rack of his folded T-shirts. She pushed herself away from the closet, slamming the doors to cut off the invasion of the synthetic smell.

Mixie gasped for fresh air, then she high-tailed it back to the dining room.

"What did you do?" she choked out. Two heads turned toward her. Nathalie's, however, stayed resolutely still, eyes focused on the jacquard-print wallpaper in front of her. Her wild-eyed stare chilled Mixie. "What did you do to him?"

"What—" her mother began.

"She knows exactly what I'm talking about," Mixie said, advancing into the room where the spirit still hovered over the steaming food. "His clothes smell like they've been soaked in some kind of . . . chemical. It's like a dry cleaners in that garage."

"Those chemicals are dangerous. Saw something about it in an old case file one time." Benjamin tapped on his phone, and after a few swipes of a finger, held the device out to his sister. "Here."

Mixie scanned the article about a chemical she couldn't pronounce. Fury rose up in her chest when she read out loud. "This says 'stays stable in drinking water, however effects can be combatted with iodine.' You cut salt out of Terrell's diet, didn't you? I remember him telling me that."

Benjamin's mouth set in a line, and mama's fingers slid back and forth over her pearls as Mixie spoke.

"'Care must be taken as continued exposure can cause arteries to clog.'" Mixie tossed the phone back to her brother. "You killed him! Why? How could you, he—" The words loved you stuck in her throat, and she couldn't force them out.

A grating rasp ebbed out of the woman, and belatedly Mixie realized it for what it was: a laugh. The tendrils contracted, bringing Nat against the table again and again, until her echoing laughter descended into a wet rattling.

"Enough!" Mixie removed her gum and pressed the lump of pink over the second candle flame, extinguishing it. The third quivered but valiantly held as the shadow receded, and Nathalie slumped to the table.

She mumbled words Mixie couldn't hear, her cheek resting on the white linen, spittle-thinned blood leaking from her mouth.

Mama called for an ambulance while Mixie leaned over to the woman's chair. Pressed her fingertips against the neck. Listened to the labored breathing. She knew enough to not move the woman until the EMTs showed up, in case there was neck or spine injury.

There was one thing bothering Mixie. She bit her lip, trying to control the urge to ask. The flavor from her gum was gone, leaving a bitter coating in her mouth. She looked up, but mama was busy blowing out the flames under the chafing dishes. Once she removed the foil trays of food from them, and Benjamin packed up, they'd be ready to go. They'd leave the door unlocked for the paramedics.

Fuck it.

Mixie leaned down, put her mouth close to the woman's ear. "Were you ever really pregnant?" she whispered.

Nat's tongue slipped out, swiped her dry lips. Her lipstick was gone, leaving a smeared rim of dark liner that made her face look unfinished. The mischievous glint in her eyes was answer enough.

"Jesus." Mixie stood up, but Nat grabbed her arm, pulled her close once again.

"Plain ol' Gatorade works every time."

Mixie yanked free, rubbed her arm to rid herself of the clammy feel of that grip.

Benjamin came around to Nat's side of the table and moved the cutlery out of her reach. He'd put the lanyard with his police badge on it around his neck. "Just in case," he said.

Mixie wasn't sure which one of his actions he was referring to, so she left it and gestured to the shadow of her ex-husband hovering in the corner, subdued but not banished. Yet.

She inhaled the scent of cinnamon on her skin. There was still truth left. She turned to the shadow hovering tableside. "Terrell, where is the deed to the house?"

Silence.

Of course, Terrell wouldn't answer, not with his less-than-favorite dessert on offer. But he was already here, already summoned, and there was no reason to waste a truth.

Mixie drained the last drops of wine from the bottle on the table and held the open mouth toward her ex-husband. "If you'll come to mama's house with me, I'll bake you a pie. Pecan this time."

After a moment, the inky shadow compressed itself, twirling down into the bottle like water running down a drain.

Maybe, Mixie thought as she inserted the cork, she'd start with changing that wallpaper.

Sweetgrass Blood

The Weaver

I BLOTTED THE BLOOD FROM MY BRAIDS WITH A HOTEL TOWEL, MAKING sure to keep the plaits in their intricate swirling pattern. The blood was viscous and sticky, and it clung to my strands like a gruesome pomade. I worked by candle light, making sure to clean my hands and nails of red before sitting down to weave. It would not do to get smudges on the baskets.

The crisp sweetgrass softened and gave under the pressure of my hand, releasing the scent of the sea at midnight. My lips, dry and cracked from lack of water, formed the words to the hex in a language that died even as I spoke it.

A part of me broke, each time I did the magic. Not my soul or my spirit—they were far too distant, far too thickened, like bark on a pecan tree. Perhaps they'd fled completely like the rest of me—my heart, my sympathies—all gone with the tide.

But no. None of those things.

I wound the strands of grass tighter, using the sharpened spoon to push them through each other, pinching where the next loop needed to be, my fingers cramped into claws, the stiff grasses leaving tiny splinters invisible to the eye but not to the flesh.

The grass was just right, pliable enough to bend but not so fresh that it leaked sap, its own blood, onto my hands. Four completed baskets lay on the floor to the left of my bare feet. This one would be the last, and it needed to be larger, to hold the head.

Weary now, I lay the basket aside and pushed myself upright. Once, I had been able to pull both of my feet into my lap, but I was no longer capable of a full lotus. Time and broken limbs had removed that ability. Now, I placed a foot on the sofa in front of me, and picked at the layer of dead skin on the sole of my foot.

It came away without resistance, a thin, diaphanous layer of my body—pale against my hands—fluttering in the wind from the box fan. Left was a tender pink layer of flesh, new, unable to withstand the tortures of the world. I stared at the circle of skin, so stark in its baby softness against the ashy roughness of my feet. I chewed it as I went outside.

In the front yard, I walked barefoot and silent. The camellia tree's leaves rustled at my approach.

"Hush, Sister," I crooned. "Just a few, my lovely, a few."

I plucked the soft, mauve petals and carried them inside. By moonlight, I returned to the weaving, my fingers soothed with the tree's scented oil.

Once the baskets were finished, and my hands were aching from hours of twisting and bending the grass to my vision, my will, I took up my stick. Holding the polished wood eased the pain, allowing me to open and close my fingers around the cloth-covered dowel. I stood with the wood's help, but once I was on my feet, I didn't need its support. With strength once again in my body, I pounded the stick on the wooden floor. Again and again, stick and pound, stick and pound, turned the house into a living, vibrating drum.

Voices of those gone from here came to me amongst the resonance. *Husha da soun'.* Warning me, protecting me as they had done for over forty years. *You brin' da poet.* I acknowledged their silent whispers with respect, inviting them to join me.

"I know. Let her come."

The Poet

The ink I used—ground by my own hand and mixed with well water—seeped into the paper. A snowy sheet of felt lay under the paper to compensate for the bleed. The brush made no sound as it flowed along the page.

Quiet. Heavy and the air is full of water. Rain will come soon.
No struggle this time.
Only shock and the swiftness of the blade.
Sweet and tough.

I signed my name, then went into the bathroom of the old plantation house I'd grown up in. A spot of dried blood lay on my cheek like a beauty mark. I left it there, enjoying the coquettish look it gave to my worn, tired face. Reconsidering, I ran a hot bath laced with the scent of vanilla and sandalwood—warming scents against the chill that seemed to be embracing me constantly—and submerged myself. As I looked up at the pinkening water, I knew this was just beginning.

Unbidden, the sound of a stick pounding into the earth reached me.

Thudding. Pounding. Rhythmic madness. Thundering into my mind, obliterating the calm I had so carefully conceived over these years. Killing it.

It was my fault that I heard it. Years ago, when I was in unruly pigtails, my grandmother had warned me.

If'n you hear your name call, make sho it me. If'n you aine sho, don' answer.

Not only had I answered, I'd done so more than once.

And now whenever they needed me, wanted me—an errand, a stalking, more even—they called. I suspected that when they wished or when I didn't answer, they entered anyway.

I submerged myself again, to drown out the sound—the stick pounding its rhythm deep into my brain. Eyes open, I stared at the widening cracks in the ceiling. The rhythm, the pounding of the stick grew, swelled, deepened until chips of paint flaked from above me, dropping into the water like dead flies. Even with the water buffeting my ears, I heard them, their voices, and I knew at some point, I'd respond.

Seconds ticked by as I lay there, the room looking murky and ethereal through the warm, still water. Respiration became a luxury I didn't need, barely wanted, as I slid slowly into unconsciousness, their songs taking the place of my breath.

When I woke again, I was on the floor of the house. The living room. Even in the sweltering heat, the hardwood floor was cool against my bare belly. I turned over onto my back, the drone of the ancient air conditioner slowly taking the place of the voices, returning me to myself. My wrists, my hands ached. I opened and closed them, staring at the brown palms before my trembling fingers covered them. One of my first thoughts was to get some polish to cover the deep, ruddy stains on my nails. Red or maybe purple or black. Then they would match the bruises on my arms.

I pushed myself to my feet, stumbling only once—twice—as I gained my footing. As I shuffled over to the kitchen, I saw them stacked up in a corner by the old, dusty console TV. Baskets, at least a half a dozen, all woven from the sweetgrass that grows alongside the ocean. I knew the shapes—you could always tell which family made the baskets from their shape, their design—and the sight of them made me itch with memory. Scratchy fibers, leaves bent until their limits were reached. My hands ached.

Thrown, I rushed past the remembrances into the kitchen, to first gulp, then splash water onto my face. It was the water, always the water that brought me back. It also helped carry my being, my mind, and my actions, away in the first place. But I couldn't live without it; it was part of me, just like they were. Escape was useless and damning.

Words rushed up at me like waves, and I scrambled to put them down. Frantic, I searched the kitchen, finally finding an old envelope to write on. My ink was elsewhere and I couldn't spare the time to look for it— the words might be gone by then, and I burned to capture them. Head spinning, heart lunging, I found a knife-sharpened pencil, eraser-less and chewed. I wrote, fingering the patch of new skin on the bottom of my foot.

> *Inside me lie oceans*
> *The sea's dead are my kin*
> *De famblee*
> *rises on buzzard's wings,*
> *feathers spouting from the stumps of pain*
> *soaring away from their bones*
> *leaving dust inside me*

I filled the envelope, turning it and writing along the edges until it was filled with gray lead. It calmed me, but not like the ink. Why hadn't I noticed it before? Only the ink took away their voices. Maybe I had noticed, but the emptiness of being cut off from everyone I had loved, those who had died for me, was too much, and I put away the revelation.

They shied away from everyone else, my people; they eschewed the written word, its documentation of their ways and thoughts.

We had never been a people to write things down. We—a mish-mash of African and Black Carib—lived by our voices, songs and tales, and they had kept us alive, had kept us apart from the outside. But I'd gone outside. To the world of poetry, of academia, of word processors and digital recorders. It was to this world I took the old ways, recorded them for others to see and hear. It was for that, and only for that, they couldn't forgive me.

It was for that and only that—they'd kill.

In a daze, I stumbled from the kitchen, back the way I came. My feet were clumsy and my ankles protested holding me upright, and they twisted from under me and I went careening into the wall of the living room, knocking into the stack of baskets. They scattered with a rustling, scrambling sound and one reedy lid slipped from its home, then another.

My mind didn't want to accept what my eyes couldn't refute. For a flash of time, I was confused, and I sank to my knees to get closer, needing to know and not wanting to. Without effort, my hand reached out to the contents, but I recoiled when I felt the Weaver's—no, my—handiwork: the slickness of blood, the putty-like texture of dead flesh. Flashes of memory peppered my vision: capture, screams, the whistle of my blade through stale air.

I was on my feet without hesitation, running into my bedroom. There, I threw open the closet door, tossed out unmatched shoes, shirts that had fallen from their hangers onto the floor. My old yoga mat from when I thought meditation would bring me peace and silence. Finally I found the roll of paper.

It was old, soft, and made of rice, a sustaining product for my people. Wound tightly, the roll was the length of my arm from shoulder to wrist. I unrolled it until it reached from one wall to the next, then down the long hallway that ran the whole of the first floor. I gathered up pencils, pens, found the pot of ink I'd made from galvanized nails and strong black tea.

Frantically, I wrote. On my hands and knees at first, then changing to a squat, then to sitting cross-legged on the floor. I wrote everything I could think of: gospel hymns, victory songs, work songs older than slavery and the pop song lyrics inspired by them. Scratched onto paper. Preserved and documented.

Ghost stories. Cautionary tales. The sounds of humming rose in my ears. The stick pounding was heavier, closer.

Your paper won't save you.

I know the Weaver's voice by now, although her weighted rasp was always accompanied by others long dead, some whispering in a chewy-sounding Gullah, some shrieking in dagger-sharp Kreyòl. There was no need to look up as I knew she was there above me, shadowy and dim but as real as the screeches, the screams. Her scent was salt: from sweat and from the ocean where her bones lay.

Down the hall I moved, ignoring the ache in my knees, the constant pop of my joints as I adjusted position. Write. That's all you have to do and this will all come to an end.

"Let me go," I managed, still inking the rice paper as quickly as I could while keeping my words legible. My fingers cramped, my back bent to the task like a sharecropper.

Our blood flows in you. Our pain, our sacrifice has made you what you are. How dare you? How dare you deny us!

"Don't make me do this anymore."

For a moment, something akin to sympathy crossed her face.

Accept our fate, Sister.

My hand only faltered a moment, a missed word, a malformed loop on a letter. The Weaver's voice was irate, and it came to me on breath that was stale and unused. But I kept writing, preserving the ways in a manner anyone would be able to grasp. The stories, the songs, the superstitions, even the reasons behind these methods of madness, I managed to scratch along the rice paper.

I was halfway down the hall now and I was getting tired. My arm at the shoulder was tight, the muscle ready, poised to jerk and spasm. But it was my knee that gave out first, sending me toppling into the pie pan of ink I'd laid out. The paper soaked it up like a bandage, obliterating some of my words and forcing me to start the entire section again. Lying on my stomach, I took up the ballpoint pen, but the paper couldn't withstand the pressure needed to make the ink flow. It tore, leaving holes in the fine ream. Where the ink spilled and softened it, my weight separated it from the rest of the roll of paper with a chilling silence.

No. Nonono.

The pencil was no better. It left no more than a specter of words on the page.

I pressed harder, turned the pencil to sweep the page in an attempt to sketch my words, but the paper wouldn't hold them. I scraped my fingers against the empty pan, trying desperately to gather enough ink to make the next letter.

My inked finger touched the paper for the tiniest moment, before the Weaver had me. As she pulled me into her embrace, I saw I'd left a fingerprint on the rice paper—like a signature.

When I came to, I couldn't move. At first, I thought it was a dream or that I had been called again by the voices and I had done—something. That I would be waking up yet again, with blood saturating my braids, leaving featherlike swirls of red on the hardwood floor. I waited for clarity to come, for the sea of fog to lift from me, and when it did, I opened my mouth to scream. It came out like the call of a buzzard. As I breathed in, I tasted the salt of the sea.

The Weaver's fingers were deft and sure as they pulled the drying sweetgrass through my skin, pressing each new row of fiber into me with the sharpened end of a spoon. Her firm tugs forced the grass to obey and it bound my fingers, silencing them. The voices were also quiet now, the stick pounded no more, but she hummed as she worked, secure in telling me secrets of my people.

Folk

IN A PLACE BEYOND FAR, MY BRAIDS ARE WOVEN INTO THE SWEETGRASS basket encasing me, and I am surrounded by the scent of the ocean and its dead. A crack of light breaches my intricate prison, and I shift, twist only a fraction, to take advantage of its brightness—there is no warmth from it.

I look at the pads of my fingertips. The flesh, bloodless, has been stripped away, and instead of muscle and meat, there is a network of twisting reeds, coiled, wound tightly into green-brown curlicues. Three of them in a staggered pattern like stepping stones in a garden. I touch my fingertips to my face and feel the prickly scrape of dried palmetto leaves.

It is the mark my people use for their handiwork—no, I lie. Only the women use it. It is the women who show their pride this way, their nimble fingers pinching and twisting the sweetgrass before forcing it over and through itself with the end of a teaspoon, whittled sharp. It is woven into their baskets, each one distinct like a signature. It is embedded in me.

Awake now, I run my blunt nails over my you-must-be-mixed-with-something skin, raising pink welts. My flesh crawls, itches, and in the dim light from the moon coming through the old plantation house window, I can see it ripple with intent.

Three circles, tightly wound, a trinity formed from one strand of sweetgrass. It isn't the Holy Trinity, but something other. The poet, the weaver, and the . . .

what? Which am I? Through the fog of interrupted sleep, I can't remember. All I want is a shower. To scrub clean, to fill my nose with scent, to rinse away the sweat and dirt and dead skin.

But for me, water brings the dead.

Grandma is an expert with the machete. The blade doesn't look like much, but they resemble each other—brown and thick and sharp-edged. Her grip is firm on the walnut handle and the blade sings briefly before severing the sugar cane on the counter, leaving a fibrous rip in the air of the stuffy kitchen. The screened door is open, as are the windows, but the breeze carries with it the sulfur of marsh and secrets.

Once, twice more, the blade falls, and then she is handing me a flat plank of cane to chew on while she teaches me the magic. I can barely see over the counter, even on my tiptoes, but I know to listen. The blue crabs in the slatted box next to me spit rhythmically and click their claws. I poke at them with an eraser less pencil, and Grandma snaps at me to stop making them tough.

She controls the machete with ease, her plump arms fleshy and loose with age. The knife comes down and up with swiftness, and a crack appears in the side of a shaggy coconut. Gran has already drained the milky liquid into a measuring cup, so she lets me try to pull apart the coarse halves of the seed. I am unable to, even with my bare foot braced against the wooden cabinet. My fingers are too soft and small for this work. But I try and try, and one day I manage it, the sound of tearing coconut meat a victory. She tells me I am ready. I can barely contain my excitement, but I know to listen.

When I think of those times, I wonder if the machete misses sinking into the sweetness of sugar cane and of coconuts. But I soothe myself with thoughts that blood can also be sweet.

I give in and turn on the shower, lulled by the sour stink of my own body. The oils I usually use to clean my skin and scalp have left a tacky layer on my body, which after a fervent scratch, lays under my fingernails in grayish clumps. The ancient air conditioner drones on, but provides little apart from ambient noise.

So I can spend as short a time in the water as possible, everything I need is already on the ledge of the bathroom window—sage shampoo, a comb, and a red net bag, which used to hold oranges, now filled with too-small bits of soap, melted together into a multi-colored waxy lump. Under the stinging hot spray, I wet the net bag and saturate my braids.

As I scrub myself, eyes closed, my thoughts wander, lulled by the bliss of the steaming water. I work shampoo between each row of plaits and almost groan at the pleasure of it. How long has it been since I enjoyed a full wash? Not just standing at the sink, sponging my important bits with a cloth.

I resolve to stop avoiding the water. Who cares if they come? So what if they take me? I always awake back here, soaked in seawater, my fingers cramped, an arthritic tightness curling my palms. What could I have done that is so soul-shaking? For days after, I sleep fitfully, bombarded with murmuring voices until the house and my mind finally go silent.

The shampoo foams white, puddles of it drop from my squeezing hands to the floor of the tub, and the swirling water thins them. I open my eyes and see the soapy bubbles running toward the drain, and it reminds me of foam-topped ocean waves as they crash against the shore. Pounding fills my head, like drums or like the cloth-wrapped stick the weaver carries that punctuates her every step. *Stick, pound. Stick, pound.*

It is then I realize I've made a mistake. Shampoo runs into my eyes, and I bite off a squeal of pain. I flail for the shower curtain, but it is not there, or my fingers cannot grasp it. Water beats on my back, and within it, between the droplets, I hear the pounding of the stick, calling to me in a language clearer than words. Soon, voices join the call—those still here and those already gone. I bless the dead and try to clear my vision, but when I peek out from my stinging eyes, the room is a swath of eggshell white filled with indistinct shapes.

The voices speak in Gullah, their words chewy and springy like the tongues speaking it find them tart but irresistible. Sometimes, the words are in Kreyòl or in Carib, but I understand the orders all the same. I fight—I always do—but the weight of history, of my ancestors in the earth and those lying beneath the sea, crushes me. I turn to the shower wall and brace myself against the slick tiles.

"Why are you doing this?" My soap-flavored whisper is drowned out by the rushing of water, now smelling of the big salt.

Fuh da famblee. Fuh oonuh.

The voices usually do not answer me when I ask questions, but this time they do, and I know to listen. I don't understand why my family, why me, but I turn my face to the salty spray, letting it wash my self-inflicted wounds, and I feel cleaner than I have in weeks.

When I finally emerge from the shower, I limp toward my bedroom, bracing myself on the doorframes. Though I'm naked, the air conditioner does not chill my flesh, and I feel no shame in my body. From the depth of the closet, I pull out a thin white dress made from cotton the voices bled for. The machete I strap to a belt on my hip. After dressing, I pull out the cloth-covered stick, thicker than a broom handle and polished smooth, and take up the call myself.

Stick and pound. Stick and pound. My feet thud against the hardwood floor, turning the old house into a living, vibrating drum. I do not sing, sure there will be enough time for that once we are together. When I am sure the call cannot go unheeded, I use the stick to support my steps down to the ocean.

There, the sweetgrass bows in the wind like geisha. I pluck the strands I need, choosing tender pieces that will bend more easily to my stiff fingers. They release their sap, coating my palms in the scent of sunbaked grass and distant shores.

When I return, I know the poet has come.

Sheets of paper made from rice, a staple food for our people, line the walls. Her handwriting is unmistakable as is the scent of her handmade ink—the tang of rust-covered galvanized nails soaked in acidic black tea. Against everything in me, I read her elegant scrawl.

> *The weaver calls with words like the tides*
> *Here, then gone*
> *A riddim*
> *Shushing my lips*
> *But blood bonds, wields the blade*
> *Under the smile of moon*
> *We fly together on buzzard's wings*
> *Returning to the ocean our bones*

For the first time I can remember, I am afraid of the poet. I grasp her paper, the feel of it is too soft, too flesh-like for my comfort. I ball up the paper in my fist, move to yank it down from the wall.

"Ah, Weaver."

Her words, languid and hoarse, emerge from the shadows to enclose me in a circle of reeking ink. I try to step out of the circle stained onto the old floorboards, but I can't. It resists any movements beyond its barrier. I touch the machete with my fingertips.

"What do you want?" My voice is more tremulous than I want it to be.

"You called me, and I am here."

"Why? I've never . . . I've—" I've done something. But I don't know what.

The words in front of me blur and run, dripping off the end of the scroll-like paper to pool on the floor just outside the circle. The ink puddle is reflective, like good patent leather. It shimmers for a moment, then the poet rises from the spill of ink to stand before me—brown skin, white dress, black fingertips.

"Fuh de famblee," she says.

A shiver takes me. "The family," I manage to scoff. "Everything is always for the family."

And it was. All I learned, from crafting the baskets to pounding the stick to calling for those who would fill them, was for the family.

I cooked for gran when she got too sick to do for herself. Morning and evening, I'd go out into the fields for food, swinging the machete to cut through watermelon vines and great handfuls of pole beans. The heat was stifling, a wall between me and comfort. Without tall trees for shade, the sun's brightness faded my vision to white. Still, I swung the blade, cutting roots and filling my basket.

When the voice came that first time, I thought it was gran calling me, and without a thought, I answered. I couldn't see her, couldn't see anything, and I ran through our fields, saying, "Yes, I'm here! Where are you?"

Gran wept when I told her what had happened. "Dey gone use you gals now. For what-so-never they wants."

I'd thought she was crazy, maybe seeing things like the old people do. "It's just me here, Gran. There's only one of me."

She shook her head as she patted my hand. "No, there ain't, baby."

We ate in silence that night. After I cleaned up, she asked me what the voices had said. I told her word for word. I told her each and every time they called what my instructions were, until she died and her voice joined the others.

"You answered them." The poet is unsympathetic, ink dripping from her intricate network of braids to make letters on the floor.

I know she's right. I should never have answered. I should have gone to a root lady to purge my mind of them once I had. *No,* I think as my hand tightens around the stick, the one I use to pound the earth, sending messages far and wide to anyone willing to hear. It's so much more than that.

I've allowed them to use me. I've opened myself to their wishes, their desires, and I've sent the call out to hundreds, maybe thousands. *This one must die.*

The poet had to die.

"And I have," she said, reading me with ease. "Fuh oonah." She held up her wrists, and I saw the marks, the pattern of slices in her skin that I recognized as my own handiwork. It is the women who show their pride this way.

"For you," she repeats in English. "You bound my hands. You silenced me. Kept me from telling our story to those who wanted to listen."

From the depths of my psyche, I remembered. Pushing the grass through her skin with the handle of a spoon, whittled sharp, as she struggled to write. Pulling it tight as she cried out, her voice the call of a buzzard's. My fingers kept working, binding her as I added strands of fragrant grass, bending them around her flailing body.

They are xenophobic, my people. Hating to be recorded, watched. Hating their words, their songs, their spells taken and shown to the world. The poet had been trying to capture these words, to put them on display for others to see. My people, a mélange of Senegal and Ivory Coast with a sprinkle of Muskogee, hide from the eyes of the world. Even so, our culture has leaked out, mostly recipes and a few stories, but even that is too much. They must stem the tide. And the poet was too large of a vessel of knowledge. She had to be contained.

The ink circle tightens.

My fingers are slick with sweat, and I fumble for the knife, but I manage to grab it. I thrust it out, expecting to meet resistance from the circle, but there is none. The blade *shicts* forward, the short jab missing its target. The next time and the next, I raise it up like gran taught me and bring it down, letting my weight add to the force of the blow.

The machete finds the poet's shoulder, her hip, but she doesn't react. My efforts rend her cotton dress, slice open her brown skin, but as with my fingertips, there is no blood. I shrink away from my handiwork this time and watch as, slowly, black patent-leather liquid pools to the surface of the poet's wounds, closing them.

Her ink continues to flow, lustrous and shimmering. It climbs the walls, seeks the paper, then crawls along it, becoming jagged characters, and finally the words to a hex that will bind us into one.

I raise my stick to pound, to call the ancestors to my aid as they've called me to theirs, and the cloth-wrapped dowel comes down with a hollow thud. Again and again, I pound the floor, adding to the vibration of the earth a different, deeper rhythm. My feet shuffle and brush the floor like a broom, bringing a melodic desperation to my song. *Stick, pound.* To the message, I add my voice, croaking and toneless though it is. I recall gran and her words, pull them closer to strengthen my plea.

For a moment, the poet sinks back, surprised. And I redouble my efforts. Then she smiles, almost tenderly, as her braids rise from her shoulders.

The plaits whip the air as if powered by a hurricane, lashing thickened ribbons of ink at me with staggering force. Icy black clings to my arms, my bare feet, my face.

"Your strongest memory cannot compare to my palest ink," she says, the whips coming faster now, coating my exposed skin. A lash of ink hits me in the mouth as I am drawing breath, and I cough, choke on the metallic bloody tang. As I taste her words, it is only now that I realize she'd written out of love . . . out of pride. And I'd crushed her.

The ink is heavy on my arms; I can barely lift them. It covers my face. The stick has fallen silent as have the ancestors.

I am alone.

Alone with the poet as she comes to stand over me, the circle allowing her entry. I want to apologize, am desperate to, but blackness coats my tongue, and only a gurgle emerges, sounding strangely like water as it drains from the tub.

My body shakes with tremors as the poet's circle recedes, returning to slip under her skin. She draws closer and embraces me as I once did her. Blind, all I can see is the dark. My fingers find the holes in her wrists, the sweetgrass under my skin unfurling, emerging to bind us together.

The poet smiles, knowing that with this she is a prophet. "I've missed you."

A Cure for Ghosts

D O YOU TOUCH WHAT ISN'T YOURS? THAT'S WHAT SHE DID.

No, no . . . Don't argue. You asked me what happened and I'm gonna tell you. You just need to listen. Listen and keep still.

Couldn't keep her hands to herself, that one. Don't you go giving me that look, gal. Your daddy might think butter won't melt in your mouth, but I know better. You can't fool the joker, baby.

Look at her. Thinks she knows everything there is to know about everything. Hmmph. She sneaks in here while I'm giving a tour . . . of these old plantation grounds, no less. She and that boyfriend of hers—who ain't got the sense he was born with, mind you—sneak upstairs into a cordoned-off room to explore. That what they call touchin' other people's belongings nowadays? Exploring?

Shouldn'ta been up there in the first place. What you think a rope 'cross a closed door means, gal? If you didn't know, I took my sweet time and printed out a sign and fixed it to that rope, good and tight, so I know you musta seen it. And what did that sign say?

That's right.

Do.

Not.

Enter.

But that don't apply to you, huh?

She and that boyfriend, they see bottles on the dresser. Real nice ones, all different shapes and sizes. Some colored glass. Others engraved or accented with graying silver. She assumes it's perfume inside those bottles and opens one to smell.

You know better now, don't ya? How do them ghosts smell? Like dirt and damp moss and dank places closed so tight no air ever enters. Like the end. Like everything and nothing.

Well, sistah . . . you in it neck deep.

If you don't know what you're doing when you open a jar, spirits escape. Attach.

Then they use you as they wish. When they wish. Usually, it's your body they want. Just the chance to be alive again. Breathe. Taste. Feel the sun and the wind and the rain on their skin.

Oh, you already found that out? You already see she's different? Then why you here, may I ask?

A cure? Ooo hoo, honey child, don't make me laugh. A cure for ghosts?

What you think this is . . . a church? A cathedral?

Got news for you. This ain't neither one of those places. So many died here, I'm surprised I don't have some of them spirits up my nose right now. Know why I don't? 'Cause I keep my hands and all my other parts to myself. 'Cause when somebody warns me, I listen.

Sir? *Sir.* I know she's your daughter, but no, I will not accept that kinda language. You can just sit on back down, 'cause you can't demand nobody to do nothing. Not me. At least not here.

What's that? You're right. She is just a child.

You're what—fifteen? Sixteen? You're twelve? Lord, and you wearing all that—never mind. I'm gonna tell you something. Spirits don't care who they ride. Children younger than you have been homes for spirits, and that ain't gonna change any time soon. Not when you go fiddling with things that ain't your business no way. I still see that little she-devil in there behind your eyes, but don't worry. She'll fade soon enough. Takes a little time. I can see her dimming as we speak.

So you're going to sue me. For what? Child endangerment? Negligence? Fine, fine. Can't wait to see the look on the lawyer's face when you say, "That woman's negligence caused my daughter to get possessed by a ghost."

Um hm. I see you hadn't thought of that.

Go on. Have her tested. Her blood pressure, pulse, body scans, brain scans . . . I'm sure those'll all turn out fine. She'll be in perfect health. Better than she was before, probably. Hard to prove damages when there's no real evidence to show the child got anything wrong with her.

I'm gonna make this last suggestion before I show you out, sir.

You had a willful, wanton daughter who was doing everything she could to make you shame. From those bags under your eyes, you were at the end of your rope before, weren't you? Now you have a daughter who is happy to be alive and happy to have a working body. She minds you. She's well behaved. I'm willing to bet things are bit easier around the house too. Think about that.

What was the suggestion? Oh, yes. Almost forgot. Enjoy the peace of mind. Take her home. Maybe even get her an ice cream on the way. You'd like that wouldn't you, gal? Bet it's been a long time. Almost eighty years? My, my. Way too long.

Let me get the door for you. No, no, it's all right, I handle heavier things every day. Uh huh. I know, you'll never stop trying to save your little girl. Yes. If I find out anything more, I'll call.

You're welcome, sir.

Take care now.

The Stringer of Wiltsburg Farm

DADDY CALLED TOBACCO A QUICK AND DIRTY CROP. QUICK BECAUSE IT was one hundred days from planting to harvest. Dirty because cutting the leaves off the plants released a juicy, dark sap that dried, sticky sweet, on the skin. Mud then clung to the sap, eventually drying to a thick crust that itched and flaked, turning brown skin ghostly gray.

Still didn't keep him from sending me out in the fields.

"It's 1949," I told him, pouring coffee from the pot on the iron stove. "Times are changing."

Daddy hobbled to the kitchen table with his horn-headed cane, weight on his good leg. He spat a thick wad of tobacco chaw into an old coffee cup and my stomach turned at the yeasty, sickly-sweet smell. Its juice stuck to his beard and he wiped it away with an arm.

"Times don't change that much, Annie Maggie. Not 'round here." He looked outside at the sun coming up over the trees, already drying the dew on the crop. "Still got leaves to cut and worms to pull."

I shuddered. I knew which job I was going to get. One of the blades from a used harvesting machine he bought from some white man upstate had come lose and torn a gash in his leg from knee to ankle. Until that healed, he couldn't be in his own fields like he wanted, cutting and pulling, chewing and spitting, alongside all his farm hands. Back bent to the tasks, sweat pouring off him like it was coming out of a bucket. Smiling all the while.

Because he couldn't get out in the fields, I couldn't keep going to school.

"You had plenny schooling, gal. More'n yuh mama or me ever had."

"I know." I tried to keep the disappointment out of my mouth. They had worked so hard to get me here where I was: almost nineteen with a few more months to go until I could get myself a diploma, then take the county test to be a teacher myself. But that would have to wait. Daddy was hurt, mama was dead, and Jeannie had gone off and gotten married.

My sister married the first man showed any interest in her. She hated the farm, the tobacco. Said the smell of the leaves drying and the manure in the fields made her sick. Daddy heard her one time and waxed her tail for talking mess about what put food on the table and clothes on her back. Jeannie never said anything else about the farm, but she grabbed onto the first boy she saw was going somewhere out of town and held on for dear life.

Her letters came every so often, talking about her crochet and house-cleaning and selling her homemade jams at the corner market. But she never visited. One of the ladies from the church went to visit her aunt up there in Neville and said she heard Jeannie yelling at her husband for smoking a cigarette. Said she wouldn't be in no house with a man that smoked. Kicked up such a fuss, he stomped out the offending stick and grabbed Jeannie's arm and dragged her home.

That left daddy and me to handle everything in those hundred days. We hired croppers for the cutting, usually five men. Including daddy, it was barely enough to get the leaves cut, bundled, dried, and to market on time.

"I don't know why you won't marry one of these men and start having some children can help us round here. They's good workers, each and ev'ry one."

"Hm."

"What's wrong with 'em? You acting like one of 'em is Tobacco Man or somethin'."

I snorted as I tied an apron around my waist. The Tobacco Man was a silly story croppers told to keep farm owners from having them out in the fields working at night. *Betta crop while the sun shines, or T'baccy Man gon' take you away. He like darkness. Come and cover you—and then you gone.*

Never did find out where the Tobacco Man was supposed to take his victims. If he was out there in the night, maybe I should go and ask him if he's seen my mama. I busied myself and had eggs, scrambled hard, along with day-old buttered biscuits and a few sausages on plates for breakfast. We ate in silence, daddy knowing I didn't like him talking about marriage and kids, but still, he did it anyway. Always thinking about what would be best for the farm.

I didn't want babies. No one I had to be responsible for. Each time I said it, he got this look of pity on his face and told me I'd change my mind about getting a teaching job. *Women were changeable,* he'd said. I'd learn. I'd be a good mother.

But I'd seen how mama declined once that baby boy she had came out stillborn. She hollered and cried, wailed long, throat-drying warbles until her grief turned her into a banshee and she flew off into the night.

Daddy never talked about that. The night he'd held onto mama's shaking body, clad in a floral cotton nightgown, as she screamed her pain. Soon, she started fading, getting thinner and lighter until we could see the whitewashed walls through her deep brown skin. Jeannie and I had just stared, unable to move, as daddy clutched at her, his big, rough hands tangling in her pressed hair and tearing her nightclothes. Soon his hands fell free all on their own, and mama slipped through the keyhole in the front door.

We all ran to the door and threw it open, calling to her, coaxing her to come back, but she was gone, the inky, starless night and the waving tobacco swallowing any trace of her. The next day, on my walk to school, I found a small piece of that flowered cotton beside the fields and put it in my bag. It was dusty, dirt-flecked, but I held it close to me.

Now, some eight years later, I'd managed to sew it into a quilt I kept on my bed. When I missed her, wished I could talk with her, I rubbed it, imagining her not as a monster but finally having the freedom and the peace from daddy's demanding ways she so desperately wanted. Even though it meant my ties to this place only got tighter.

I put our empty dishes in the sink as daddy took a drink of medicine from the amber bottle a root doctor gave him. He had never been fond of hospitals. They tended to turn Negroes away, so he kept his ailments close to his chest and called on local healers when he couldn't stand any more.

As I took off my apron and put on my boots—handed down from an old pair of daddy's—he asked me, "You goin' stringing when the men get here?"

Of course, I was. He wasn't going to spend the money to hire a woman to tie up the bundles of tobacco leaves to sell when I had two good, nimble hands and a strong back. I nodded. "Gotta pick first though. Then I'll feed the chickens."

Daddy grunted. The medicine was already taking effect. I checked the bandages on his mauled leg before he shuffled to the sofa. "You're a good girl, Annie Maggie."

I picked up the tin bucket next to the door as I left.

"Yeah," I mumbled. "Too good."

The day was already blister hot and rising. The chickens in the yard warbled and clucked while they scooted around my feet. I tossed out a small handful of corn from the pocket of my dungarees, enough to whet their appetites. I'd be back with supplemental food in a while.

"You'll have to wait for the rest, ladies. And gentleman." The rooster stared at me with one unblinking eye, then tilted his head away as though he had better things to ogle.

I marched out to the furthest row from the house and bent to the task. Thankfully, it hadn't rained last night or the job would be worse. Peering close to the tobacco, I reached out and grabbed a fat cutworm, then pulled it from the stalk. It wriggled in my grasp, its multitude of legs waving as it roiled. A deep brown stain of tobacco sap showed where the creature's mouth was. I dropped it into the bucket and moved to the next one, hoping I was out early enough to mitigate the damage of the worms' feast.

Left alone, these cutworms—caterpillars, actually, fat-bodied with stumpy legs and an endless appetite—could destroy a crop in less than half the time it took to harvest. So someone had to remove them. Pesticides were no good. They killed every other bug except these worms, which remained unharmed by the chemicals, and continued to glut themselves on the soft leaves. And those chemicals couldn't be washed out either. The tobacco got cut, strung, hauled, and dried with no worry for the killing liquids.

We knew other farmers who had tried to do without pesticides, and what little of their crop remained after the bugs and beetles didn't garner much at the sales. Most of the buyers swore they could taste the difference in flavor, and they didn't like the look of the leaves, chewed into lace by the insects. Those farmers didn't break even, and they didn't go without the chemicals again.

Daddy usually did the pulling, his wide fingers the same thickness as the bright-green worms. He would pull three or four in succession, keeping their wriggling enclosed in his palm, before dropping them all into the bucket. He said he couldn't even feel them struggling.

I felt them wriggling against my palm and trying to squirm through my fingers. One of them bit my hand, right where the thumb and first finger meet. The pain was at first a pinch, then it blossomed into a full stabbing that shot up my arm to my heart. I let loose a curse, yanking off the offender and crushing its body in my fingers. I threw it in the dirt, ground it under my heel until it disappeared into the muck.

For a few moments, I sucked on the wound, the metal-sharp taste of my blood strong. Out here in the middle of the ripening leaves, the worms were all I could hear. The symphony of thousands of mouths chewing, devouring the tender leaves, surrounded me whenever I was out in the fields. Moist snapping, followed by the scent of wet leaves, musk oil flowers, and manure-rich dirt. At times like this, I understood Jeannie more than I would ever tell her.

I pressed my lips together and went back to my task, pulling off the destructive cutworms one after the other, moving backward down the row of plants. Their softness hit the bottom of the tin bucket with a sick clunk. Pulling until the clunk turned into a gentler plop, meaning the worms were piling up, plump bodies cushioning the fall of their brothers. Soon, they'd be able to wriggle toward the lip of the bucket and out, determined to get back to the plants and feed.

They get addicted to it, one cropper named Ray Earl told me when I first started helping daddy after mama left, as a young girl about ten or so.

"Them worms get used to that t'baccy, you know. Gets to where they won't eat nothin' else, even if ya gib it to 'em. They do anything for that there weed."

Back then, he was about the age I am now, barrel-broad in the chest with legs that looked too skinny to hold him upright. He slipped a piece of cut cane between his lips and sucked. "Dat's why you neber gon' see me wit none of it."

And I didn't. Every evening after the croppers had their meal, most of them sat on the porch outside with a piece of leaf from the day's cuttings. The men were filthy, covered in dark sap dusted over with mud and muck, but still they sat wiping spittle from their chins and yacking away until dusk, their chewing loud as the worms.

Ray Earl would get his pay, thank me and Jeannie kindly, then head off to wherever it was he lived. He'd be back the next morning, ready to work. He was the one who told me about Tobacco Man.

I laughed to myself as I pulled more of the destructive worms. I'd believed every word he'd said. Looking up at him, seeing his rough brown hands darkened even further by the clinging sap and edged with a line of powdery ashiness on the knuckles, fascinated me.

Know why you 'posed to wait 'til sunup to start with t'baccy?

I shook my head, pigtails bobbing.

'Cause that's when T'baccy Man go to sleep. Don't want him catchin' you, huh?

I'd screamed a little, and he turned serious eyes on me. *Don' worry, Annie Maggie. He aine gonna git you s'long as I's here.*

I think I'd been a little in love with him then. But he must've gotten killed in the war soon after because he never came back to our farm after that harvest. I'd forgotten about him and his story. Strange how things come back.

The bucket was about a third full. I hefted it in one hand after wrapping a dishtowel around the handle to protect my hands. After so little time in the fields, my hands had gotten soft, unused to the hard labor of daddy's harvesting.

I trudged back to the house, leaning slightly as I balanced the weight of the bucket full of wriggling worms. Some tried to crawl away. I shook the bucket, jostling them so they tumbled back down to await their fate.

Back in the yard, the chickens swarmed me, *tuck-tuck-tucking* the food call to each other, somehow aware that I was pulling today instead of Daddy. I shook the bucket, sprinkling the worms in a narrow line through the middle of the brood. The birds pounced, scrabbling for the bloated worms, their toenails scratching the work leather on my boots as they rushed to glut themselves.

One of the birds, a frizzle hen, was scratching in another part of the yard. I went over to look and saw a dusty square of cloth. I shooed the black-feathered bird away and knelt to look at what it had uncovered. A red felt bag tied with coarse twine—a mojo hand. I backed away, almost dropping the bucket. I was no root lady, but I knew what to stay away from.

I peeked inside to ask daddy, but he was snoring on the sofa, fast asleep from the pain medicine. No help there. I saw some of the workers coming toward the house, the younger boys who came with their daddies to work the crops, their slim fingers pinching off the tobacco flowers as they began to grow. Some boys were given small knives to cut away the stunted, unproductive leaves, so the larger ones could flourish.

One brown boy stood near the water pump in the yard, getting a drink, and I called to him.

"Young man," I asked. "You know where Dr. Beetle lives?"

He looked at me with a frown, his pouty little mouth dropping water. "Dat root man? Yeah, I know."

Of course, most of us did. Conjure healers were the only medicine we had sometimes, except for the granny remedies that were shared between us to cure the most everyday ailments: sick stomachs, heat stroke, women's heavy monthlies. Plucking leaves, boiling tea into tonic, healing poultices for cuts and scrapes—it was big business. The one thing croppers didn't have to worry about was flies and mosquitoes. Insects couldn't abide the smell of the sap.

"Please get him for me," I said, already reaching into my pocket for payment for his quick feet. I handed him a coin and a piece of peanut candy I'd made, wrapped in waxed paper. "Tell him I found something."

The boy looked at me while he unwrapped the candy. He popped the square into his mouth, then turned and took off, running for all he was worth through the dirt and empty wooden poles standing upright in the fields.

I sighed, knowing those empty poles were down to me to fill. I walked to the nearest one in my borrowed boots, pulling a roll of string from my pocket. I tied together the stacks of leaves the cutters had left, then hung them on the poles for the wagon to gather, keeping an eye out for Dr. Beetle's arrival.

The short, thin man chuckled when he saw the mojo hand in the yard. "This what your hen scratch up, eh? Who you trying to get?"

I never messed with magic, making it or buying it, and I told him so. I was going to school, so I wouldn't have to live my life worrying about who was laying tricks on me or hexing my family. Teaching was a suitable job, and I'd send money to daddy whenever I could, but these fields full of their caterpillar worms and black sap-coated superstition wasn't for me.

"It's a protection mojo. Nothing wrong with a little help now and then." He looked up at me through his blue-lensed sunglasses and adjusted his hat to shade his eyes. "You could use some help, ain't that so?"

"No, thank you. Daddy will be up and around soon, and things'll go back to normal. All we have to do is get through this harvest and sale. We'll be all right."

"No shame in asking for help, young lady."

I bristled at his tone and the words themselves but held my poise. "You're right. When I need help, I'll surely ask for it. I called you here today, didn't I?"

Dr. Beetle folded his frail arms across his bird-like chest. He looked directly in my face for long moments, making me uncomfortable with seeing my refection in the blue lenses. "That you did. You getting along, then? Got enough workers?"

"We're managing all right."

He ran his tongue, pink as trout flesh, over his bottom lip. "Uh huh. How's Jesse?"

"Daddy's fine. You can go see him if you like. He's inside."

With a nod, the doctor shoved his hands in his pockets and headed for the house.

"What do I do with this thing?" I pointed to the dusty, worn pouch in the dirt. The chickens had finished feeding, but were giving it a wide berth.

Halfway in the door, he turned back. "Bury it right back where it was."

I frowned. "Why? Nobody here needs protecting."

"Now how would you know that, Annie Maggie?" He stepped the rest of the way in the house and shut the door.

I grabbed a sturdy chicken feather from the ground and used it to pick up the bag. I carried it to the drying shed and dumped it into the fire.

That night, a wet mouth met mine in the dark. Smoky, slick-soft flesh slid across my body and I rose to meet it, pressing deeper into the tender recesses. It was like no other kiss I'd had, not from any of the croppers, not from the other girls at school who liked to pretend they were kissing each other to practice for when a boy wanted them. This was a feast, falling into a nothingness made of our tongues and mouths. The night prevented me from seeing anything, and I reached out, sure it was a dream, only to feel the stiff brush of leaves under my fingers. I heard breath—felt it—my own and another's, huffing soft bursts of heat in the chilled night. I tasted sweetness, felt the tiny, welcome pain as teeth nipped at my lips.

I tugged on the leaves, tough as fabric in my hands, wanting to be closer, to feel this swirling madness, this ache pulsing low in me. From a distance, I heard my name, whispered at first, then louder until it rang out, breaking the daze I was in. I sat up in the darkness, shuddered at the cool dew seeping through my nightgown. Lights went on in the house upstairs, first one, then a long time later another. Daddy was moving around on his own, calling for me.

"Annie Maggie!" Daddy's voice called again, rising with his fear of not finding me.

When I put my hands to the ground to push myself up, leaves clung to my sticky palms. I yanked them off, jumped to my feet, and raced for the house. I made as little noise as possible getting in, still unsure how I'd ended up outside in the fields. We kept a mirror on the wall right inside the door to stop ghosts entering. As I passed, I caught a glimpse of my reflection.

My hair was wild, loosened from the braid I wore it in to sleep. But what made the cry wedge in my throat was the dark brown stain covering my mouth. I reached out and brought my sticky, dirt-covered fingers to my lips, wincing as they made contact. They came away coated in cedar-red, the color of blood and sap. My lips stung.

Daddy let loose a string of curses when he saw me. "Answer me when I calls you, girl. You think you too old for me to whip, but—" His voice died when I turned to face him, and a sound like a wail from behind a pressing hand escaped. Eyes round as moons, daddy backed away, hitting his side against the buffet table, hard. He didn't even flinch, not even as fresh blood began to seep from the previously white bandage on his leg. Not until I started toward him.

He held his walking cane out to stop me.

"What you been out in them fields doin', girl?" As I tried to stammer a reply, he answered for me. "Out there rolling around with that . . . thing?"

"What thing?"

He slammed the cane down on the hardwood floor, and I jumped at the sound of cracking wood. "Don't play wit' me, girl! You know good and damn well what I'm talking 'bout."

I shook my head, then tried to smooth out the snarls in my hair, managing to make the tumble of straight and coiled strands worse. My fingers trembled, and I winced as I drew the damp sleeve of my nightgown over my mouth to wipe away the blood and sap.

Daddy's eyes were shining, full of held-in tears. He turned his head up to the ceiling and trails of water ran down his cheeks.

"No, no, no!" he shouted. "I lost Marie to that thing, and I damn sure ain't gonna lose my child to it."

I didn't know if his words were for me or for himself or for God, and I didn't care. "What about mama?"

He looked at me as if he'd forgotten I was there. His lips quivered, and he let out a whimper.

"She left, Daddy. She left that night 'cause the wailing called her, and she had to go. The grief was too much because she wanted a boy baby so bad."

Daddy shook his head. Tears flowed freely down his brown face, leaving streaks of salt white.

"No, what?"

He didn't answer me, but I heard him babbling. *Mercy* and *Jesus* were the only words I could make out.

"You might as well tell me." I stepped forward, but he moved away from me, back down the hallway toward the stairs. I pursued, knowing what I looked like and not caring. Not anymore. "Tell me, Daddy! About mama—what happened?"

"You was only a child. You and your sister."

He leaned back against the wall, slid down it to thud into a sitting position on the floor. Behind him, a smear of blood from the soaked bandage stained the whitewash.

Fury rose in me, burning the back of my throat and filling it with the taste of smoke and ash. My voice pitched up, rising, shaking the framed pictures of me and Jeannie that stood on the table. "Now, Daddy!"

"She couldn't have no boy child. Just you girls. I wouldn't—I wouldn't let her rest until she had one."

The taste of tobacco sap rose in my mouth, sweet and smoke green, familiar as a lover's kiss.

"If she couldn't have a boy, I tol' her . . . I tol' her she could find somewhere else to go. To keep the farm going. To carry on the Wiltsburg name." His words came thick and fast, trying to explain, to get me to see.

All I saw was red.

With one wave of my hand, I swept the pictures from the table, glass shattering at my bare feet.

"I thought you loved her!" My scream shook the boards of the house. From far away, I heard a wail, full of lonely fury.

Daddy seemed to rally at that, losing some of the fear that had crept into his face. "I loved her! It was her that step out on me!"

"What?"

"After she gone, I saw that boy baby. Ain't look nothing like me." He spat the words out like he would a plug of chew that had lost its flavor. His shadow flickered and grew behind him. "Looked same as that ol' cropper thought he was too good to stay 'round after meals."

"Roy Earl?"

I felt the bottom drop out of my stomach, the taste of bile and green tobacco rose, sour-sweet. I stepped forward again, the shards of glass biting deep.

"Yeah, yeah. I showed him that boy, told him I knew . . . I knew what he was doing with my wife." Dark spittle dribbled from his chin, but he didn't bother to wipe it away. "I put both of 'em in the ground that night. Both of 'em."

I watched the shadow grow denser, deeper. The smell of the tobacco leaves grew, weeping out from that dimness.

"That's why I set that mojo hand. Protect you from me. You and your sister." His leg wept openly now, the red blood darkening to a syrupy brown. "It didn't hold."

"Dear God," I whispered. "You're him. You're Tobacco Man."

His eyes rolled, whites stark against his skin. His words were back to a babble as the shadow covered him, cloaking him in smoky darkness. "Best for the leaves. Best for the farm."

"Stop."

"Boys stay. Girls leave. Boys . . ."

"Stop it, Daddy."

"Best boys. For the farm. Best boys. Girls don't—"

"Shut up!" I screamed, the wail opening my mouth larger than should be possible. Cutworms poured from my lips, plopping and plunking down to the hardwood floor, their segmented bodies writhing and rolling to right themselves. My scream cut through the still night, waking the chickens, who joined my wail with their insistent, fear-ridden cackle.

The worms swarmed toward my daddy, crawling over each other in a desperate attempt to reach him, mouths already working, chewing. His shadow pulled away from the wall and swam over him, cloaking his body in heavy dark. Leaves rustled, wet with dew and something denser that dropped to the floor in fat plops.

Daddy shuddered, but he didn't try to get away. He knew who had come for him. And I knew what that buried nation sack had been for. My throat was dry, raw, and still I hollered. The worms fell faster, more than I'd ever seen in my life. They reached the tobacco-scented shadow covering daddy, and they pulled, tore at it, chewing . . . always hungry. Always chewing.

I could see through my transparent skin to the swarm of bright-green creatures on the floorboard, gnawing. Another wail came from across the fields, and the sound of mama's voice brought tears to my eyes.

My wail stuttered to a stop, and I fell against the banister to the second floor, panting. I held onto it as I walked upstairs to my room, avoiding the crush of writhing cutworms feeding on their favorite meal. I slept.

When I came down the next morning with my bags packed, daddy didn't ask where I was going. He just looked at me, diminished from his usual upright stance and nodded.

"Bye, Daddy." I walked away, down the front steps and across the fields, to the bus stop that would take me into town. I didn't look back.

I learned he died a few years later, and I returned to the farm to sell it off. Jeannie said she had a husband and three kids to look after, but she would do her best to attend. I had his body cremated after harvest and sprinkled his ashes over the tobacco fields he loved.

For the last time, I took cord from my pocket and tied up stacks of leaves and let the bank have the proceeds from the sale. The farm itself, and all the equipment, I sold before returning to my starter home and my own classroom of kids. Jeannie never made it back to help me tie up the loose ends, but she happily took the check I offered.

She Shells

AUNTIE TALIKA MOLTS ONCE A YEAR AND NEEDS A SAFE PLACE TO HIDE, to heal, before she ventures out into the cold waters again. She usually spends this time—about a month, sometimes more—with me. It is the only time I ever see her anymore.

I run my fingers through her hair, removing the tangles formed as she thrashed and flailed to free herself of her old body, which lies next to her on the floor of my conservatory.

I resist the urge to nudge her thin, translucent carapace away from me while I tend to her hair. A replica of my aunt in gossamer, face upturned toward me, toward the light; it unsettles me, even after seeing it countless times. Sunlight reflects off the face of her discarded shellskin, making the mouth look as though it's smirking at me. The back has been torn open, clawed out from the inside, and its edges blossom open like sharp-edged petals.

My fingers retain the slick slip of the candlenut butter and peach oil I use on her tresses. I rub my hands together, awed at how different they feel, how much softer. Like auntie's new body, grub soft, and giving. It's also grub white and I know she hates to see herself this way. She won't look into a mirror or the clear sea until her cells release color, first in tiny irregular circles, covering her body in faux freckles, then spreading into a uniform shade of deep brown. Then, it will harden into her new shellskin.

Then she will leave.

But for now, I take care of her.

I tug too hard on her braid and she hisses, baring sharp, pointed teeth set between bruise-purple lips. I know from experience her uncovered flesh is sensitive to even the slightest pressure. I swallow my sigh. My hands gentle against her scalp, the only apology I will offer.

"Talika," I ask. She doesn't like for me to call her by her title of Auntie. "Did my mother ever comb my hair?"

"Yessss . . ." Her words come out on a sputter of breath. "Many, many timessss."

"Tell me . . . I want to remember."

My auntie's lisp forms the words to a tale about my mother and I am drawn in. Into a memory that somehow belongs to all the ancestors, yet is still mine alone. A story of scales and snakes and stone. One of sisters, before meddling gods begat troublesome daughters. I stiffen at the tale. Myths are never kind, but reality is far crueler.

While she speaks, I smooth my palms over her plaits and conjure a memory of my own. I was voted festival queen when I was fifteen, due to receive a crown and sash and all the customary regalia fitting of such a title. Even had a local seamstress sew me a dress. Auntie broke my arm off at the elbow joint three days before the ceremony. Threw it into the back garden for the birds to tear apart.

"Rely on your brain, dear. Not your looksss," she said. "Don't be like your mother."

My arm grew back, of course, but it took the rest of the summer, and I stayed indoors hiding from the other children.

Auntie called the seamstress and had her put long sleeves on the dress, paying the woman extra for her trouble. But I never wore it. Eventually moths ate holes in the gauzy fabric, and I ripped it into shreds. One of those shreds was near my hand, a scrap I dusted with, the glimmer of the cloth long gone. How easy would it be to twirl it around auntie's neck?

My hands curled into fists.

"I'm going to bed. Can I get you anything before I go?" My every cell oozes with the insincerity of my words. "Food or drink?"

"No, thank you," she says, breaking off a piece of her old exoskeleton and shoving it between her lips.

I turn and leave the room, flee from the sound of teeth on bone.

Upstairs, I wipe my oiled hands up and down my arms, feeling the small ridge where my new arm sprouted. It aches sometimes, when storms hover over the sea. Funny how the ache grows after each molt.

Sleep doesn't come. Thirst does, along with the desire for this month to pass quickly. I tiptoe downstairs, intent on filling a glass with dark wine.

Hot sobs echo off the glass walls of the conservatory, condensing against the glass and running in rivulets down its surface. I ease closer on my human-like feet, silent.

Auntie Talika's segmented body now lies in a shallow pool of tears. Her abandoned shellskin, half eaten, is floating far out of reach across the room. The molt makes not only her body tender, but her soul. I approach with care, dipping my hand in her tears to moisten it before I place it on her new-skin shoulder.

Unbidden, I remember the day my mother died. Talika held me as I cried, her mouth parts clicking soft reassurances. Her tongue touched my tears, taking them into herself, while she rocked me against her chest. I fell asleep to the sound of her heartbeat, the sound of ocean waves. There were no words to comfort me, and she gave me none.

"I'm sssorry I couldn't keep her alive forever," she cries. "Your mother wasss much better than me. Your mother would have been kinder, gentler. You needed—" Her words ebb away like tides.

I kneel in the soft saltwater and pull her to my own breast. I offer her no words because there are none. I hold her gently, the only acceptance of her apology I can give. We weep together silently, filling the conservatory with tears, our hearts thumping the beat of the sea.

Room and
Board Included,
Demonology Extra

A T THE START OF HURRICANE SEASON, OUR HOUSE WOULD GET UP AND
move inland. Most of the time it stayed where it was, its oystershell
frame crouched in the middle of Charleston Harbor, surrounded by
lapping waters the color of collard-green liquor. But when the air grew thick and
electric with ozone, filling with dense, wet clouds that meant hurricanes were
coming. The house sensed this even before we did. It swayed gently, rocking
from side to side, and stretched up, lifting its long stilts, spindly as crab legs,
and headed to safety.

Once settled, the house would crouch down into the moist dirt, nestling in
to weather the storms. There we would spend the rest of the season, secure in
our little house until the weather calmed again.

When the season was over, our house would rise up, shake like a wet puppy,
and stomp back to the water. In those few months, August to November, we
would rent our extra rooms to people who didn't have anywhere safe to weather
the storms.

As a nine-year-old, I thought we were rich, having a place we could let other
people use for a while. At least we had enough to share with others, even if we
did charge them for it. Our rooms were few but nice—came with a poster bed
covered in clean sheets off the line, a desk and chair, plus a hot breakfast.

Mama had her hoodoo parlor and receiving room downstairs, right before you got to the dining room and the kitchen. The bedrooms we rented were upstairs, along with my room and mama's.

People would stay until the storm passed over, usually a couple of days, before returning to where they came from to clean up, repair, and get on with their lives. Most of the time, they were all good people, happy to have a clean room and hot meals and to let me and mama take care of them for a short while.

Most of the time.

One morning a few weeks into the season, I woke up crying. Hot tears poured down my face. I gasped for breath, my chest heaving. I clutched the bedcovers, trying to control my sobbing. But there was no way. It grew so big inside me that it finally burst, and I had to let it all out.

I didn't know what it was; I wasn't sad at all. I'd had a good summer, and so far, even with the hurricanes coming off and on, it had been a good school year. I'd met lots of people, and mama had made lots of money. Enough to last us through the winter. But this crying . . . where did it come from? Soul deep loss and pain. I got visions from time to time, which Mama said I would one day learn to control, but today wasn't that day.

As much as I tried to be quiet, my sobs were loud enough for her to hear as she walked past my door on her way to make breakfast. She opened the door and came in, gathering me up in her arms. She smelled like she always did: good, clean Ivory soap, a touch of scalp oil, and cherry vanilla lotion.

"Jamie Lou, what is it, baby?" she asked. "What happened?"

"I don't know!" I choked out. "I don't know whose pain this is."

Mama rocked me in her arms back and forth until I calmed down. She wiped my face with a handkerchief. "It's okay. It's okay. You always was a sensitive child. Always wanting the right thing for people."

"But why not do the right thing? Why not help others when they need it?"

She patted me on the back a little too roughly, but it was her way and a comfort. "People don't always do what's right if they ain't forced to. They don't wanna take the time, or they feel like it ain't worth their while."

Pain still rolled inside me, stinging and burning. But I wiped my face, swallowed the morning air. My eyes felt puffy, the skin around them sticky and tender. "But someone is really hurt."

"It was only a dream, baby."

I wasn't sure. But I wanted to believe she was right, so I rubbed my eyes with my palms, smearing away the last of my tears. When I dreamed, I could remember bits and pieces of what I'd seen, but this morning, there was nothing except a lingering feeling of wrong. Sometimes I picked up other people's visions instead of my own. Things that couldn't be in this world. Things that made my skin crawl and my scalp itch, so I tried to forget about them. Mama was teaching me to focus, but I hadn't quite got the hang of it.

"Come on, get up now, Jamie Lou," mama said. She opened my blinds, letting the welcome, white-hot rays of sun pierce through the blue sky and into my room. With a sky like that, it was hard to see how I could have been crying so hard a few moments before. "Let's get you something to drink and some breakfast. You'll feel better."

After lunch, a hurricane crept up without warning to beat the Carolina coast, headed toward us. As mama rushed to get us ready, a man came scuttling up to the front door, fighting the pre-storm winds. He had his face tucked into his shoulder, and he held his hat on with one hand. The other hand clutched a road-weary leather case.

This man was skinny and dark like me. And he smelled like my gramma used to say old Southern gentlemen did: bay rum and Royal Crown hair pomade and lots of spray starch. His clothes were still wrinkled though, like he'd been on the road a long time. When there was a gap in the wind's blustering breath, he looked up at us on the porch. Round spectacles with blue lenses—blue lenses!—covered his eyes.

"Afternoon, ma'am," he said, flashing us a hint of gold when he opened his mouth. "May I?"

Mama nodded, and he stepped up onto the porch with long, spidery legs—hovered in the corner next to the banister like a spider too—and smoothed his straightened hair. He told Mama that he was traveling and had been on the road a long time, exactly like I'd thought. I smiled to myself, pleased at guessing right. I hadn't yet come into my second sight real good, and I didn't always trust it, but I was pretty good at putting myself in other people's shoes, trying to be understanding.

The man introduced himself proper to mama and me, earning himself a bit more respect in her esteem, as Doctor Bug. She ushered him inside, closed the door behind him.

"How long you planning on staying?" mama asked.

Even though Dr. Bug was tired, he tried to smile. It looked like a real one, but it took all the rest of his energy. "Oh, long as I can, I expect," he replied.

"For now, let's call it a week." He handed over enough money for two weeks and waved off mama's argument.

"For your trouble. I didn't book a room in advance, and I expect you got enough to get you and your chile through this hurricane, not planning on having any guests, until it blows over."

Mama nodded, handed me the key to room three. "Go on, Jamie Lou. Take the man's bags."

He let me take his big, leather case without any protest, and I thought he might believe I was a boy. I looked like one with my white T-shirt and overalls and my close-cut hair. Mama never had time to oil and braid long, thick hair, so she kept mine cut short. I didn't care. Never liked the fuss over hair and things.

Dr. Bug followed me up the stairs as I hauled the huge bag to room three.

"Your bag sure is heavy."

"I'm sorry," he said, surprisin' the hell outta me. "I should have carried it myself."

"No problem. I do it all the time." I peered at him with a squint in my eyes. "What's in there?"

"Just necessities."

I unlocked room three and handed over the key.

Dr. Bug's eyes grew large. He froze up like he'd seen a snake coiled up, on the edge of striking.

"That's a four-poster," he said, pointing.

I nodded. "Yes, sir."

"You got any rooms without a poster bed?"

"No, sir. All our beds are posters. Mama says they're the fanciest ones, and people tend to like 'em. Makes them feel special."

I looked up at him. It seemed a long, long way, almost like he was towering over me. But a tower that wasn't quite straight, one that leans slightly to the side, making his shadow on the floor bent and awkward-looking.

He trembled a bit. "Fanciest ones," he repeated. Dr. Bug stared at the bed like he was thinking of what to do next.

"You don't like 'em then? Why not?"

"Too much of a . . . perch." He blinked, and the pleasant look was back on his face. "I'll have to make do, I guess. Or don't you have a room without a bed a'tall?"

Now why would you want that? I shook my head. "No, sir. Mama ain't going to let you sleep on her kitchen floor."

Dr. Bug shrugged and tossed his hand on the bed. "Don't worry. It'll be all right. It'll have to be all right."

I couldn't understand what he didn't like about the four-poster. It was beautiful, dark wood, and mama had me keep it polished to a high gloss. Mahogany, I think it was. The headboard was smooth and undamaged even though it had belonged to my great, great, grandmother. Most people oohed and ahhed when they saw this room but not Dr. Bug. He seemed unsettled and unhappy.

"Okay, if you're sure." I walked into the room, set his bag on the floor. "If you need anything, let me know."

He looked like he might have been trying to come up with something to say, but mama called me. It was time to help her make an extra portion for dinner.

Dr. Bug wasn't a sleeper. I knew because his room was right next to mine, and I heard him moving around. Whispering, scratching on what sounded like a washboard. I made up stories about what he could be doing. That rustling sound could be him practicing some kind of mystical martial art. That scratching could be him writing with one of those old-fashioned quill pens that need the bottle of ink to work. But what would he be writing? About his life, of course. His patients and all the people he'd saved in his lifetime.

I pressed my ear up against the wall between us to hear better, and I could have sworn I heard him stop. Then after a moment start back up again, scratching and rumbling and mumbling to himself.

It didn't keep me up because I wasn't a sleeper either. My visions would come at odd times, some sweet but most scary. I'd wake up after the first two or three, my skin itching and crawling. And I'd have to get a dry brush and rub myself all over to calm down. Mama said the visions would slow down once I'd been having them a while. She said I'd then have to go through something like it when my lady time started, a few months of unpredictable before it all settled down to what it was supposed to be.

Those early days of my visions set me up to be able to work all day on about four hours of sleep a night. The rest of the time, I'd read or go around the house on tiptoe, making a list of what we needed from the market or what needed repairing. Sometimes I'd draw or play the little banjo someone left in one of the rooms long ago. Quick, strong fingers could only help me.

I stayed there with my ear pressed against the wall, listening until I fell asleep, and the only visions I had that night were my own.

The next morning, I was up early. I lit the stove and put water on to boil for coffee. When I heard the stairs creak, I thought mama was coming down to get breakfast started.

It wasn't. Dr. Bug stood in the doorway to the kitchen like he wasn't sure he should come in or not.

"You can have a seat," I said. "Only coffee is ready right now. Mama don't let me cook for guests. 'Cept eggs. I can fix those."

Dr. Bug shuddered. "Coffee's fine, thank you." He slid into the farthest seat at the table. He wore a suit, not the one he had on the night before, but this one had the same scent. He was clean-shaven, and his hair was slicked down into waves.

I set the sugar dish and milk jug on the table, but he drank his coffee black while I added two spoons of each to my cup.

"So what do you do around this place?" he asked, glancing around the room.

I stirred. "What mama tells me to mostly. I'm a kid."

He nodded like he understood being a kid was a job by itself. "But you have dreams, don't you?"

I nearly jumped in my seat when he said it before I realized he wasn't talking about my sight. "Not really."

"There's nothing in this life that you really have your heart set on doing?"

The stairs creaked again, and I looked toward them. It was mama's footstep pattern; her heels made a certain noise on the carpet. When I looked back, Dr. Bug and the coffee cup were gone, the steam from his coffee still rising in a swirl like a tornado.

"Morning, Jamie Lou." Mama looked happy after a night of rest, and she smiled at me as she poured a cup of coffee. "You were up early. And made coffee too? I appreciate it."

"You're welcome." I always felt good when mama praised me. Not that she didn't do it often enough, but there was a deep, open part of me that seemed to constantly need filling with her love and appreciation. It was just the two of us, always had been, and I wanted to do all I could for her.

"Our guest joining us for breakfast?"

"I don't think so. He had his coffee earlier, but"—*What do I say?*—"he took it and left."

"Back up to his room?"

"Um, yes. I think so."

"Well, this storm is nothing to play with. I hope he made a smart decision and carried himself on back to his room. The way these hurricanes just turn up outta nowhere nowadays. Never know when you might get caught out." Mama pulled back the curtain in the kitchen and peered out the window. "Doesn't look too bad. But I think there might be something off in the distance."

"He seems like he can take care of himself."

"And how would you know that? You sounding so grown lately." Mama looked at me over her shoulder. "Let's get some breakfast in you."

I picked up the container of eggs and opened it. They were all either milk-white or toasty brown. All of them except one. I had to look at it closely to make sure it wasn't my eyes fooling me. One of the eggs had a slightly blue tint to it. The shell seemed thinner, almost like I could see through it. "Mama, one of these eggs looks blue."

"Blue? Let me see." Mama glanced over. "That's just light playing tricks. Nothing to worry about. It's a plain old white egg." She sat a pan on the stove, added a pat of butter, and adjusted the flame.

Maybe I was still unsettled from my crying yesterday, but there was something not right about that egg, and I knew it. I leaned over to look at it in its casing next to all of the other eggs. I picked the egg up, holding it to the light streaming through the twitched-back curtain. An indigo-dark blob of something swirled inside. As I peered closer, that blue pushed against the shell toward me, cracking it.

I yelped and dropped the egg. I watched helplessly as it tumbled, the entire shell shattering on the countertop and the indigo mass spreading out like ink. Mama turned from the stove.

"Jamie Lou! This is why I don't let you cook without me. Now go get a kitchen towel and clean this up. Save that egg. We can't afford to throw away food around here."

I grabbed paper towels—two, three, four of them—sure I would need that many to mop up the dark stain. But when I turned back, the blue blob was gone. Only the clear whitish part of the egg and the yellow bubble of yolk remained.

Where had it gone? Was it my imagination? I touched the egg white with my finger, pressed into the slick jelly.

I plucked up the broken shell and dumped it into the trash. Then I cupped my hand around the egg splattered on the counter, scooped it into a small bowl, and handed it to mama. With half of the paper towels, I wiped the counter clean. I sprayed it with cleaner and used the rest of the towels to remove all traces of the curious egg. I cracked the window to let the overwhelming scent of pine escape.

"You sit at that table there until I put your breakfast in front of you," Mama said, cracking another egg into the pot and laying thick slices of bread into a skillet to toast. "Drink your coffee and stay out of trouble until at least I can get some food in you. Then you can help me prepare the house for the storm."

I sat, waited for my breakfast.

I poked at the eggs while I munched on buttered white toast.

"I know you ain't leaving my good food to go in the trash." Mama glared down at me, and under the weight of her gaze, I shoved scrambled egg onto my remaining toast and forced it down with gulps of sweet coffee until my plate was clean.

Hurricane preparation was more than the house up and running for high ground. We still had to protect it, keep it from getting hurt. We also had to make sure we had what we needed in case we got cut off from help: oil for lamps, candles, matches, and lots of water.

Mama was nailing up thin boards to the windows outside to protect them against flying objects like rocks, trees, and pieces of house that the storm might throw our way. Our house wasn't like some of the newer homes, made of springy material that absorbed the blows storms dealt. I yanked the plastic foot mat out of the tub in the bathroom next to my room and rolled it up, securing it with a rubber band. Then I scrubbed the tub clean on my knees, rinsing it out three good times before wiping around the lip. I lifted the latch to close the drain and filled the tub with clean, cold water, enough to last us a few weeks if we were careful. Just in case.

To test it, I scooped up a handful and drank. It was cool but not cold, and there was no trace of the cleanser I used. Mama got to the bathroom window with her panels of wood, and darkness fell inside the room. Scrabbling came from nearby, probably mama searching for nails, but it had sounded more joyful than she usually was.

I grabbed the mat and left the bathroom. There was still more to do.

The storm came that night. Howling winds muffled the sounds coming from Dr. Bug's room, but I heard them still. I kneeled on my bed, my ear against the drywall, and listened. Scraping sounds, chipping sounds, and the occasional curse. Finally, around three in the morning, the sounds stopped. The bed creaked, and I heard the deepest, longest sigh ever. I settled down too, for some reason feeling strangely comforted.

Winds still howled outside in the morning. I was up before mama, the three hours of sleep enough to refresh me. The house was darker with the windows covered, even though it was morning. Sand and dirt battered the walls and the freshly applied boards. Something metal, a paint can or a bucket clattered down the road. Water splattered in the bathroom next door to my room, like it had been hit with a flat hand. I crept closer, still in my pj's but with enough sense to put on my sneakers in case I needed to run. I glanced over to room three at the other end of the hall. The door was closed, no sound or movement within. Guess Dr. Bug needed more sleep than I did.

At the bathroom door, I listened. The splat came again, a patter of bouncy rhythm like a baby playing in a washtub. Then a gurgle. A leak maybe? Another customer mama had signed in without me knowing? I swung the door open, flicked on the overhead light.

From the corner of my eye, I saw a flash of color. Black and blue sliding by faster than my sight could catch. There and gone. I turned, but I was alone in the bathroom. The sounds, the splashes and gurgling, had stopped. I approached the tub, peered inside. Ripples ebbed away from the surface, and a feather, long and sharp, floated in tight circles.

What bird could have gotten in here? Had to have been before we boarded the house up. But where had it come from? I plucked the feather from the water, and it left a faint, oily blue outline of itself before dispersing. My stomach boiled. I wrapped the feather in a piece of paper towel and shoved it in my pocket. After, I drained the tub and got back on my knees to scrub it clean again.

Dr. Bug missed his morning coffee. It wasn't worried, knowing he'd been up all night. I wasn't sure why mama hadn't heard his maneuverings, must have been the sound of the screaming wind and the roar of the ocean. I so wanted to watch the waves during the hurricanes. From the news on our battery-powered radio, they got to be twenty feet or more. Churning waters rising up like a hand and smacking the daylights outta the shore—that would be a sight to see. But I couldn't. Couldn't do much of anything, and I got bored and restless. It was the worst thing about being cooped up in the house during the hurricanes.

Once when I was real young and mama was sleeping during a storm, I slid out from her bed. I took a broom handle and knocked loose the hook on the back door. Rain hissed from the concrete-gray clouds, the sound like sizzling on a hot plate. Lightning cracked, splitting the sky in three parts. When the thunder boomed, it echoed in my chest, shaking the house. I held my arms out to let the sound fill me up, let the hurricane feed me its energy. I felt whole, safe, the cracks of loneliness inside me filling and sealing up like they were never there. Right as I was about to open my mouth and holler out my thanks, mama grabbed me around the arms and dragged me inside. She shook me as she kneeled down and yelled in my face.

"What the hell you doing, girl? Don't you ever scare me like that no more in life! You coulda killed your fool self. Lighting woulda struck you dead."

Her words bounced off me. I heard, I understood, but she didn't need to worry. The storm was a protection of sorts. A safety. No one would come to hurt me while it raged.

I took the feather from my pocket. Unwrapped the paper towel, now with a smear of oily stain. The hurricane still roared outside, rain pelting the roof and porch. Daylight was weak as used dishwater, the sun unable to brighten the day. Mama had gone to balance her books, which meant she had poured herself a Tom Collins and sat down at her desk with her ledger and sign-in books.

"If Dr. Bug gets up, you tell him there's biscuits on the counter and cold meat and cheese in the fridge there. If he can't make it to meals, I don't cook on call." Then she paused, probably remembering he paid for two weeks up front. "Make him a fresh pot of coffee if he wants it."

"Yes, Mama."

Only, he didn't get up. I did my chores, read a book, strummed on the little banjo. Fed up with all of that, I pulled the feather from my pocket again, twirled it around by the tip. It was sometime around noon, according to the stove clock, and I journeyed upstairs to check on him. His door was cracked open, the scent of fresh-cut wood leaking out. I peeked around the door. The room was dim inside, only a little light shining through the edges of the window where mama had cut the boards too small, but the room seemed to be empty. I nudged it open more, calling,

"Sir? I mean, Doctor? You in here?"

No answer.

I flicked on the light, watched the house's lights trickle from the vein that ran the length of the wall up to the ceiling and down to hang over the middle of the room. I staggered back when I saw it.

Mama's four-poster was ruined. Images were carved into the formerly smooth surface of the wood. Vines and flowers wound their way across the head and footboards and twined around each post of the bed. Deep gouges in the dark wood revealed a paler color to the edges of the raised images. The floor was littered with wood chips and shavings.

It was beautiful and fearsome at the same time. An entire story played out before me in wood, light and dark, smeared with what looked like shoe polish and blood:

A man walked in a forest of low-hanging trees. He stumbled on an egg, breaking it. He kicked away the shell, angry at it having stained his shoes and clothing. That same man running as an enormous bird chased him until he left the forest.

"What in the world—" I said.

"It's my story."

I whirled around to face Dr. Bug. His straightened hair was still damp from his wash, and he'd slicked it down so good, I could see the tracks of the comb. Yet another suit, only this one looked easy and comfortable, a long way away from the look on his face. His eyes without their lenses looked watery and nervous.

Before he could see, I slipped the feather up the sleeve of my shirt. "You broke an egg."

He nodded, his face all serious. "And that thing been chasing me ever since."

"The mama?" I didn't even bother to wait for the doctor's answer. "Yeah, they're like that when you do somethin' to their babies."

"Well, the storm is on us now, so she won't be able to fly here. Plus, y'all got the place boarded up and secure, so she can't get in." He came into the room, put his blue glasses back on. "I'll be moving on after it passes over. Won't leave you all to deal with her."

"Who is she?" I felt a bit sorry for her, who'd lost her baby because of the doctor's carelessness. Maybe her egg was like me, the only child she could ever have. 'Cause of Dr. Bug, she would be alone forever.

"Who knows? Doesn't matter, no way. I'm gonna get ridda her one of these days."

I cocked my head. "Kill her?" He messed up *her* egg, and he wanted to get rid of the bird mama for being mad? He had some kinda nerve.

"If I have to. If I can." Dr. Bug sat on the bed, the mattress dipping under his slight weight.

The feather tickled, but I didn't dare scratch or pick at it in case it grabbed his attention. "How are you gonna do that?"

"Been tryin' for what feels like ages now. Best I can do is to keep moving until I figure it out." His eyes were fiery behind the cool-blue lenses. "And I will, I promise you that."

A sharp jab stung me under my shirt. I yipped at the pain, but it passed quick.

"You okay, girl?" He was staring at me curious-like.

"I'm fine," I said, rubbing my arm. I had the urge to smash the whole bed to pieces. Crush the entire story of what brought Dr. Bug here. When mama found out . . . I shuddered just thinking about it. "But mama ain't gonna be happy about her bed."

At least Dr. Bug looked like he felt bad. "I know, and I'm sorry for that, but any kind of bed raised off the floor will bring her to me that much quicker. Doing the carvings gets me a little more time."

"Well, you gonna have to tell mama you did it and why because I sure don't want all of that on my head."

He packed his tools back into a leather case. "I sure will, young miss. I surely will."

"And you gonna have to pay for it," I said, meaning the bed.

"Don't I know it," he said, seemingly meaning something else. His eyes shifted to the carving of the bird. Its face was a little bit human and a lot furious.

A rush of wind shook the house to its foundations, and it groaned. I turned away to head back to my room. "Coffee's downstairs if you want it."

The storm raged on for most of the day. Rain on the roof sounded like stones clattering when dropped from above. Thunder backhanded the sky. The lights flickered and went out, leaving the house dim and riddled with shadows. Wind shrieked so loud, I had to ask mama to repeat herself twice, making her snap at me.

"I said, 'Are you finished cleaning the rooms?'"

"Oh! Yes, ma'am." I hadn't cleaned Dr. Bug's room. The sight of the carvings and the beautiful damage to mama's bed had stopped me.

Mama hadn't cooked. When power went out, we ate whatever would go bad soonest without being kept cold. I touched the eggs in their cardboard container, but they would be okay for a long while. By candlelight, mama and I shared the rest of the crab rice from the night before and sloshed extra milk in our coffee. The scent of melting wax and fried bacon wafted through the room. Still no appearance from the doctor.

"I know you frustrated you can't go outside and burn off some energy, but we're in here for the duration. Go on and do something with yourself 'til this storm is over." Mama tucked a crossword puzzle book under her arm, grabbed her pitcher of Tom Collins, and sat in her recliner. She worked the puzzle by the light of a hurricane lamp, pushing the tip of the pencil against her tongue as she thought. Likely, she'd doze off until her stomach or her bladder got her up. Sometime after nightfall, she'd make her way to her bedroom.

I felt so deeply for her, in this house with only me for company. Aching in the arches of my feet made me toe my sneakers off and leave them in the hallway. Wind shrieked banshee-loud, tossing and rattling whatever was outside, and the rain sounded like loads of gravel getting dumped on us, but the oystershell house held on.

Barefoot, I slid upstairs to check on Dr. Bug. His door was closed but unlocked. When I peered in, he was stretched out on the bed, snoring. A tiny piece of foil lay in an ashtray, surrounded by ash. Sweat beaded on his top lip and forehead, and his mouth worked as if he was mumbling in his sleep.

Inside . . .

The thought spoke to me like a trusted friend, and I moved quietly forward, closing the door behind me. I could smell the storm in this room, and I saw he'd lifted the window a bit and used one of his woodworking tools to bend and crack away a piece of the board mama put up to keep us safe. A large-enough piece for him to look outside. Rain drizzled in, speckling the sill and dribbling down the wall. Anger at his disregard for our property dug into me. He thought nothing of what belonged to others.

I spat on the doorframe, over and over, thick spit that sealed the exit closed. Turning to the bed, I pulled up my sleeves, careful of the feathers that now sprouted there. I stalked across the room, careful to avoid any of the floorboards that might creak and give me away. My toes grew longer and spread wide, the baby one melting together with the fourth. I hopped up on the footboard and squatted. One toe on each foot rotated backward to balance me as I perched.

"Doctor," I called to him.

He groaned in his sleep, fussed, smacked his lips. I clutched the footboard tighter. A crack began to split the wood, spidering outward. At the sound, Dr. Bug shook his head, inched up on his elbows. Our gazes met. He opened his mouth to scream, but I spat again, cutting his cry off before it could develop.

"You broke her egg," I told him. "You need to apologize for that."

I couldn't understand most of his babbling through the sticky muzzle. I reached over with my still-me arms and scooped his mouth clear. He was so scared. I shifted on the footboard, my claws scraping the wood. "Do the right thing and maybe you can leave here."

He rolled from the bed to try and get out the door, but it wouldn't move even though he yanked at it with all his body weight. He raced to the window to pry off the boards with his fingers. Finally, he slumped down to the floor, his back against the wall, whimpering and shaking his head. His tears mixed with my spit into a gloopy mess. I joined him on the floor. He'd had his chance.

I clawed open his belly just enough to place a new egg inside. The storm covered most of his screams, but I wasn't worried about getting in trouble. Once mama saw how the doctor destroyed her bed, she'd agree that I'd done the right thing.

Crickets Sing
for Naomi

IF THESE DANGGONE CRICKETS DON'T STOP FOLLOWING ME," NAOMI grumbled as the insect bounded out of the path of her wedge heel. Another of the bugs scuttled across the top of her foot, its spiny legs pricking her exposed skin. Under the streetlight, moths danced in the circle of brightness on the otherwise dim road. Heat ebbed from the asphalt, making her wish she'd worn flip-flops.

For months, the insects had followed her around. At her parents' house, one had even jumped out of her pocketbook onto the hardwood floor. While her mother screamed and leapt onto a chair, her father had chuckled, scooped up the invader, and placed it outside.

Deja blew a bubble, the pink gum garish against her black lipstick. Once it reached the size of a tennis ball, she sucked the bubble back into her mouth with a silence-rending crack. "Know why, ennit?" she asked, working an acrylic nail under the bra strap biting into her shoulder. "You. It's all you and your Afro-Asiatic, trans-continental—"

"Okay, okay. Leave it alone." She'd had enough commentary on her parentage when she was in school. Black mother, Korean father in the middle of the race-obsessed Bible Belt, add to that thick glasses, pimply skin . . . it all served to make her the object of scrutiny and ridicule. But ten years later? Unacceptable.

Still. At least she hadn't brought up any of the older, more insensitive nicknames. She could still remember Deja pounding her fists into the belly of that ashy-skinned lil boy who yanked her glasses off that time after school while they were waiting for the city bus. Maybe that was part of the reason she was out here with her now, quaking under the 'round midnight heat. Duty. Payback.

Damn.

A car rolled by, not slowing, headlights a sickly yellow-beige that barely cut through the tarry night. Another followed it.

"Ain't they supposed to be lucky anyway? If you catch one or something?"

A tiny chitinous body thumped into Naomi's arm before falling away, feeling like a reprimand—her mother's finger flicking against the tender inside of her elbow to get her to pay attention in church. She'd turned her eyes to Reverend Parker's squat, sweating form clad in folds of blue and gold robes and let her mind drift. From the frantic waving of her fan, she was sure her mother wasn't fooled, but to everyone else nestled on the padded pews, it looked like she was rapt.

"What, crickets?" Naomi rubbed her hands over her upper arms to chafe away the feel of the scrabbling legs. "Yeah, they're lucky. And not just in Asian culture. African too."

A third vehicle, a sun-bleached silver van, inched up to the corner, then stopped. The engine gave a rough purring cough as it idled, puffs of charcoal-tinged smoke adding to the mugginess of the night.

Deja nudged her, then headed toward it, her freshly plaited braids snatched back from her forehead so tight, she was the one who looked Blasian. "Then you couldn't escape it. Come on."

Escape was on her mind right now. Could she manage to keep Deja's friendship if she just turned tail and hauled ass back to her car? She'd parked it off the road at her friend's request, near a thick growth of saw palmetto leaves to obscure it from prying eyes. After that they'd had a ten-minute walk to the corner, facing Old Mister Ronnie's red dot. Naomi could use a red dot right now; she'd had her fill of Deja's tight-lipped pleas for her company. She'd rather be wandering the store's narrow aisles filled with dust-laced bottles of liquor and mixers, planning what kind of concoction would put her out of her misery for the night.

Instead, she tore her eyes away from the now-empty shop. Mister Ronnie had died years ago, and no one else had been able to make that location work.

It stood alone and decaying, flakes of paint clinging to the worn boards, telling of more prosperous times.

Naomi followed her friend's confident stride over to the silver van, staying a few steps behind. Who went up to a strange van parked on the roadside at night? She wished she'd thought to bring the jang do her father had given her. The small knife would have brought her some comfort.

No one got out of the van, but the engine turned off, ending the rumbling purr. Deja pulled the handle of the back door, and it opened, releasing a waft of nag champa incense to sit on the air. She had one foot in when she looked back at Naomi. "You coming?"

If it had just been about the ashy-legged boy, she might have said no. But Deja had also grabbed the loop of her backpack as she wandered the sidewalk, the world a pale wash of watercolor without her glasses, and yanked her back from the corner. A moment later, a truck sped by, honking angrily. She'd sat there on the sidewalk, dazed until Deja placed her glasses in her hands, and the world came into focus again.

"Yeah, I'm coming."

Naomi rushed to catch up, her shoes crunching on the roadside gravel like molars on bone. "Wait," she loud-whispered. "Girl, are you crazy? What are we doing here?"

"Trust me, okay?" Her friend's eyes glistened under the streetlights, and she waved away the gnats drawn to the moisture clinging there.

Exhaust-hot air from the honking truck sped over her bare arm, pebbles striking her face and neck like miniature buckshot. Naomi tried in vain to wipe away the memory.

"Okay."

Inside the back of the van, rich and deep with shadows, were a worn, red velvet sofa and a tan leather recliner. Deja plunked herself down on the far end of the sofa and patted the cushion next to her, which carried the scent of desperation-born sweat and aged farts. Suppressing her revulsion, Naomi perched next to Deja, keeping her weight on the balls of her feet in case she needed to spring away.

A grunt came from the front of the van. Another echoed as the passenger's seat came crashing down to lie flat, allowing the woman to pull her stooped, frail self toward the back of the van. Naomi tensed, and Deja's hand came down on her thigh, stilling her. The heat that ebbed from her hand was due to the temperature in the enclosed space. Without the air conditioner running, sticky moisture quickly built up. At that moment, Naomi knew this wasn't her friend's first visit.

"How you gals doing tonight?" Once settled in the recliner, the woman lost her fragile look, and her voice was strong for one so physically small. Her skin was soft-looking, loosening on her skull, like a well-used, brown paper bag.

Each of them muttered a greeting.

"So why are you here with me?" The old woman retrieved a pipe from a compartment in the armchair and lit it using a lighter from the voluminous folds of her dress. She took a long pull and closed her eyes, letting the smell of leathery tobacco and spicy anise surround them.

Deja cleared her throat. "I need advice, Miz Alethia." When the woman didn't comment, she continued. "I need to get rid of someone. From my life."

Miz Alethia's eyes moved under her closed, slack-fleshed lids but Naomi felt the weight of her gaze, knowing and mighty. It stirred something in her mind and for a moment, the cricket song that followed her everywhere swelled. *Hush now,* she thought, and the chirping music waned to its normal ambient sound. She could almost hear the question on the old woman's lips and was less than surprised when she voiced it.

"A woman?"

"No," Deja said, looking down at her chipped toenail polish. "A man."

The old woman's eyes rolled again, hidden under the soft-looking skin, around and around like dropped coins. Finally, the disconcerting movement stopped, but her eyes stayed shut. "What I tell you the last time, gal?"

Silence.

"Huh?" The question whipcracked out, and both girls jumped.

"To stay away from men for one year," Deja whispered.

"How long it been now?"

After a speedy finger count, the reply came. "Three months."

Naomi put her fingers to her lips. Had it been that long since Deja stopped seeing Derrick? Lately, her friend had been spending more time with her— window shopping followed by lunch on most Saturdays, but she hadn't chalked that up to her avoiding male contact. Sometimes they'd watch a movie at her house on Sunday evenings, Deja eating the leftover dinner from Naomi's mother while Naomi made cookies to ship out to her dad the next day. She'd been so happy for her friend's company that she hadn't realized she was a substitution.

The old woman leaned back in her recliner, her feet in house slippers now higher than her waist. "And what had happen?"

"My old boyfriend wants me back. He's been coming around and I . . . gave in."

"What?" Naomi shouted. "After all he did to you? Why?" Broken dates, broken promises, a broken heart that Deja refused to acknowledge. She never voiced her fears or doubts, leading all around her to believe her life was fine.

"I can't just turn off my feelings. Not everybody is as cold as you," Deja snapped, her razored brows scrunching toward each other in a frown. "When was the last time you felt anything between your legs?"

Naomi's open mouth slammed closed so hard her teeth rattled. She pressed her lips together until they felt bloodless and dead while heat rushed to her face. She pushed herself up from the low-backed sofa and headed for the van's door.

"Peace, child." Miz Alethia's fingertips brushed her arm. The tender voice and the gentle grip stopped her haste to leave. "Go, sit up front. Go on now. We gone talk in a minute."

Naomi turned. Saw Deja's profile stony and still, focused on her lap. Deja crossed her legs away from Naomi, then picked at a worn spot on the velvet nap. Saw Miz Alethia's hands on the arm rests of the recliner and wondered what was wrapped around her wrist. A cord of some sort.

She clomped in her wedge heels to the driver's seat, contorting herself to slide between both women without touching either of them. She sat sideways, legs splayed around the gear shift, so she could see smoke curl from the pipe and the tip of Deja's shoe as she slipped it on and off her foot.

"I don't know. I was . . . was . . . lonely, I guess." Deja's voice hardened. "You didn't say to stay away from men I'd already been with. I figured that was already a done deal."

A smile was on the woman's crinkled lips, baring her tiny square teeth around the pipe. "I told you to stay away from man for the year entire. This Derrick, he named 'man'?" She didn't wait for a response. "I see he is. And now you see he ain't the one for you. What you want me to do that I ain't already done?"

"Give me another chance. Please."

"Another chance to waste my good medicine?"

"No, ma'am." Deja's voice cracked.

Naomi's resolve almost did too. But she steeled herself against the feeling. She'd wait for this to be over—she'd never really leave Deja here alone—but she wasn't going to put up with that comment. She deserved an apology.

"Every time I see him now, I just want him gone. I know I messed up, but—"

The tinkle of glass sounded. "Drink this."

"What's in it?" Deja asked.

"Exactly what I put in it. Now go home and do what I say this time."

Deja mumbled an agreement. The back door to the van opened and Naomi felt fresh air wash through the vehicle. She fidgeted in the seat, trying to lift and bend her legs to get out of the awkward sitting position. Just as she twisted herself to face forward in the driver's seat, she heard Miz Alethia's voice.

"Child?"

Naomi froze, the brightness of cricket song loud in her ears. "Yes, ma'am?"

"Now, that gal can't seem to help but chase man. You got to help her, hear?" The gentle nudge of tobacco smoke accompanied the woman's words and she sat upright in the chair.

"But she—"

"Said some stuff you was wondering 'bout yourself. That potion won't do nothing to that gal. I'ma tell you what it will do." She opened her eyes.

Naomi was struck to see how unusual they were—mid-brown irises with a halo of blue where the white joined the brown. But it was Naomi's eyes that widened as Miz Alethia described her plans. Surrounded by the power flowing from the woman, she listened, mouth open.

"You got all that?"

"Yes, ma'am."

Miz Alethia patted her hand. "Now you call me when she drinks that potion."

Naomi's mind reeled from the deluge of information. "What's your number?"

"Ain't got one."

"Then how can I call you?"

"Send one of your babies for me."

"Babies?" She glanced in the direction the woman pointed and saw a semi-circle of crickets—probably twenty or thirty—climbing and crawling over each other under a flickering street light. "Oh, they're not mine. They just keep following me for some reason."

Her soft chuckle was rough, yet musical. "That means they yours, gal. Care for 'em, feed 'em, love 'em. And they'll heed you. Now, g'won. I got places to get."

Naomi hopped out of the van and trudged to catch up with Deja. When she looked back, the van was still there, emitting its contented purr, although she couldn't recall hearing the engine turn over. She caught up and the girls walked together in silence to Naomi's car. With the remote, Naomi unlocked both doors and she was halfway inside before Deja spoke.

"I'm really sorry. You know . . . about what I said."

"Yeah."

"I don't think of you like that. Cold. I was . . . I don't know."

Naomi couldn't see the van when she looked again, but maybe they were too far away. "Let's not talk about it right now, okay? Let's just get you back home so you can"—she waved a hand at the bottle clutched in Deja's fist— "do your thing."

"Okay." She didn't speak again until Naomi dropped her off at her house. "Thanks for coming with me. For everything really."

Naomi nodded, waited until Deja had unlocked her door and gone inside. Once she saw the outside light flick on and off twice, she drove away. A cricket plopped onto the now empty passenger seat, turned around, then leapt to the floorboards.

"I know," she said, through gritted teeth. "I should have forgiven her. But I'm not ready, okay? Leave me alone."

When she got to her apartment some ten minutes later, she poured a glass of plum wine and plopped on the couch. After two rounds of searching through channels, she gave up and put the TV on mute. She stared at the flickering screen, unseeing, lost in the events of the night. Movement on the floor caught her eye.

Two of those damned bugs were playing leapfrog on her I-had-to-force-the-landlord-to-update-it beige carpet. But Naomi was too tired, too mentally exhausted to protest or shoo them away. Instead, she drained her wineglass, then refilled it and returned to the couch. What kind of foolishness was this plan of Miz Alethia's?

And why did she always have to be the one helping everyone? No one helped her. Well, she corrected herself, except Deja, those two times. She sipped at the sweet, room-temperature wine. When was payback ever enough? Go to work, come home, relax. That's all she wanted to do. And have movie night at home when dad got back from deployment. Why did she have to get involved with the crazy messes her friend loved leaping into headfirst? At least, Deja was never alone.

"Ugh, I could use some company myself right now."

Another cricket jumped across the carpeting. She watched it, lazy-eyed and slightly buzzed, as it traveled across the floor toward her. It hopped up on the couch next to her, right in the middle of the cushion. It rubbed its tiny wings against each other, producing a soft, high-pitched melody.

"Don't suppose you have any solutions?" The cricket wasn't forthcoming, its attention seemingly focused on the flickering images on the screen and playing its shirring song. "Figures."

But the insect stayed where it was, next to her, until Naomi went to bed.

Naomi's cell rang three days later at five in the evening. Deja. That girl knew the bakery closed at this time. Shoulda called days ago. Had she not taken the potion? Her boss gave her a cutting look, so she sucked her teeth and pressed Ignore.

She ignored the next three calls as well, instead cleaning down the counters and the floors before leaving through the back door to empty the trash. On her way to her car, she handed a bag of imperfect eclairs to a homeless man who had set up residence near a dumpster. He grunted at her and tore open the bag.

Why didn't she care that he hadn't thanked her, or even expect it? The thought stayed with her as she navigated the knock-off-time traffic. She took the exit to the complex where Deja lived. From the parking lot, she returned her call.

"Naomi! Thank you, Jesus. Where are you?"

The frenetic voice made her pause. "Outside," she admitted.

An instant later, the door to Deja's townhouse swung open, and the line went dead.

When she got to the door, Deja grabbed her arm and yanked her inside. All of the windows were open, but the sheer curtains were closed. Air flooded in through gaps in the cloth.

"What the he—" Naomi's shout of outrage ended when she saw the body on the living room floor. "Don't you dare tell me that's dead," she ground out.

"I think so." Deja, barefoot, paced the floor. The ancient refrigerator hummed, adding to gentle insect night song.

"You think so? You didn't check?"

"How am I supposed to check?"

"Feel for his pulse. Is he breathing?"

Her friend's neck jerked back as if she'd slapped her. "Touch him? You crazy? I don't think so."

"You didn't have a problem touching him last week." Naomi pursed her lips.

Deja put a hand on her hip. "Bi—"

"Fine. Then why'd you call me?"

"I didn't know what else to do." Her gaze skittered around the room, as if looking for an escape.

"Besides kill your ex-boyfriend? I could think of a few things."

"No, I just . . . he came over when I was doing the spell Miz Alethia gave me and things got out of hand."

Naomi bent down to look at Derrick's limp form, ready to spring away if he stirred. "I don't see any blood or cuts or anything. What exactly happened?" When Deja didn't answer, she looked up. "Girl. What did you do?"

"Nothing!" She sucked at her teeth, then admitted, "I kissed him."

"Kissed? I don't kill men and I can't get one to kiss me."

"That's 'cause you dress like somebody's gramma. Who wears twin sets when they're under twenty-five?"

After cutting her eyes, Naomi dropped the subject. "Details on what happened, please?"

Deja straddled a folding chair and draped her arms over the back. "I drank the potion Miz Alethia gave me. Just as I finished it, the doorbell rang and it was him." She gestured to her ex on the floor. "I was cool and told him we were done. He laughed, so I said I meant it this time. For real, for real. So he gives me this long, deep soul kiss."

"And then . . . dead?"

"Yup," she said, teeth clicking against her acrylic fingernail. "No strangling, no fighting. Just dead."

"Damn." Naomi sat on the end of Deja's chaise longue as a chorus began in a corner of the living room.

Her friend looked up, around. "What is that? It sounds . . . like angels. Oh Lord, is God calling me home?"

"You are so extra." Naomi laughed for the first time since she answered her friend's call. "No, that's my crickets singing."

"They're yours now? You talk to them?"

"Yeah, I do." Naomi's humor softened into a smile and she realized it was the first time she had claimed the tiny insects.

Miz Alethia's words echoed in her mind, *Send one of your babies for me*. It had never occurred to her until that night they would take instruction. She'd begun simply, calling them, asking them to sing until she fell asleep. Now she supposed was the ultimate test.

Naomi whistled and clicked her tongue, and the cricket chorus came forward, hopping from corners and emerging from underneath curtains.

"Which of you remembers Miz Alethia? With the silver van? Tell her to meet me at my place in an hour, please." A few of them hopped away toward the door.

Then she ran into Deja's kitchen and returned with two pairs of yellow rubber gloves, one of which she threw at her friend. "I'll pull around back. Help me get him in the car."

Back at Naomi's apartment, they hauled Derrick from the passenger seat. With one of his arms over each of their shoulders, they heaved him up and walk-dragged him to the front door like he'd had too much to drink. Never had Naomi been so glad most of her neighbors were elderly. Once five o'clock hit, and the *Murder She Wrote* reruns were on, no one was outside.

As Naomi wrestled with her keys, the sun-bleached silver van pulled up. The old woman eased herself out and shuffled over in her house slippers.

"Evenin', gals. You called?"

Deja, for once was speechless, but Naomi had found purpose.

"Yes, ma'am. Will you come in, please?" She unlocked the door and shoved it open with a hip, then she and Deja pulled the man upstairs and inside. Several crickets bounded across the rug to investigate. "Thanks, girl. I'll call you."

"What? Call me? Why—"

Miz Alethia held up an age-worn hand. "Best if you wasn't around for a bit, gal. While we work, you see?"

Deja looked like she was going to protest more, but decided against it. "Yeah. I'ma get the bus home. Um . . . lemme know, okay?" She ran down the stairs.

When Naomi heard the door to the apartment building open, then close, she shut her door and locked it. "So how do we do this?"

"First, turn 'im over. I'm too old to be lifting man 'round."

With some effort, she got him flipped over, flat on his back. Miz Alethia looked at his face, poked it. The flesh held the indentation of her finger.

"Your potion worked."

"Always do," Miz Alethia said. The couch cricket whirred and chirped, pranced the length of the cushion. "Now you just hold on. Hold your water." To Naomi she said, "Please for a pillow."

Miz Alethia lowered herself slowly to the heap of pillows Naomi piled on the floor. She took the man's face in her lap, pulling and tugging at the flesh. It gave under her gnarled fingers, softening like clay, and she smoothed it into something—no, someone—new. His myriad of tattoos she covered by working the skin-clay taken from his face over his biceps and pectorals. The scars and discolorations on his legs and feet got a similar treatment. She encircled his penis with a firm, business-like grip and changed its look as well.

The old lady sat back. "That's all I can do. Hands ain't what they used to be."

"I hope I can do this." Naomi took a deep breath, whistled, clicked her tongue. The couch cricket hurried forward, bounced from its cushion to the arm of the sofa, then to her palm. She pushed the man's mouth and teeth open with her other hand, lowered her baby to the still warm cheek. The cricket crawled up and, after a brief pause on the full bottom lip, entered the mouth. A tiny bulge showed its progress down the throat.

The women waited.

Soon, the man coughed. Flailed. Struggled to get up.

As he sat there, a bewildered expression on his new face, Miz Alethia smiled. "Whatcha think?"

"He's perfect."

"Haven't heard from you in while. You been okay?" Naomi took the last tray of brownies from her oven.

Even through the phone, she could hear Deja's caught-in-the-act tone. "I know, I know. I should've called you, but I've been so busy."

"Doing what?"

"Working," came her too-quick reply.

"Ah, I understand that." After a few more minutes of small talk and side-stepping of questions, Naomi realized her friend wasn't going to reveal anything more. "Well, come to dinner sometime soon. Dad is back home, so mom's been cooking huge dinners on Sundays."

"Okay. Maybe this Sunday?"

"Sure. Any time, you know that." Just as Naomi was about to hang up, she heard Deja whisper something. "Sorry, I didn't catch that."

"I said, 'Can I bring a guest?'"

"'Course you can."

"It's just that I met someone, and it's been going really well. I'd . . . like y'all to meet him. He's so great—tall, handsome, sweet. And Lord, can he sing!"

How It Feels on the Tongue

CARLA SLICED OPEN HER LAST RUBY RED GRAPEFRUIT ALONG ITS equator. Ran the sharp, serrated blade around the perimeter of the ripe fruit and down to separate each juicy segment from its brother, its sister, its mate. She planned to pop the husband into her mouth and let his dying liquid hydrate her parched tongue while his wife looked on, her acidic screams silent in the sunny kitchen.

She felt like Cronus, huge and powerful, eating of his own fruit, one child at a time. Neither she nor the Titan ate out of hunger but out of fear and desperation.

As she removed the seeds from each dripping hemisphere, she noticed one had split, its crooked stalk of birth emerging from the rigid husk. The beige shell had given way to the insistent nudging of the delicate, bright-green sprout inside.

Pessimistic, she planted the seed, sure that it would die like everything else she'd attempted to cultivate. No lush job, no fruitful marriage, no fertile womb—a barren existence soured further by loneliness.

The seedling paid no attention to her past failures. In its ignorance, it continued to thrive in the grey stone pot on the front porch. It wobbled and stretched; it reached upward and pulled itself toward the sky.

Hope broke through the dusty soil of her heart, and she began to speak to the little tree—about the nasty email from her boss, the rude man at the train station who pushed past her to take the last available seat. Even told it about the property maintenance man who never missed an opportunity to make a cruel comment about what he saw as her physical shortcomings.

One evening as she arrived at her apartment home, he saw her in the parking lot and jeered, his laugh braying and nasal. The plant shuddered with outrage at the offense, losing a few sweet-tart-scented flowers in the process. Its empathy soothed her, and she touched the tip of a leaf with her ring finger.

The next day, a blue-aproned boy at the garden center answered her question about the best fertilizer for citrus trees. "They love organic."

But she couldn't leave the store. A neglected grapevine had its long tendrils wrapped around her waist. She untangled herself and gave the vine a gentle pat as she answered its inaudible plea.

As she lifted her purchase from the car, she cringed at a familiar laugh. He watched her struggle with the heavy pot until she got it on the back patio next to the young tree.

When his heavy footsteps landed on her stairs, she scurried inside and locked the door. She didn't bother to investigate his muffled screams until all of his struggling subsided. Long enough to uncork a bottle of red and let it breathe.

On the back patio, in the spring afternoon sunshine, her lush plants bookended a dried-out husk. It crumbled to powder when she stepped over it to reach for the ruby-red globe hanging from one of the tree's branches. Sangria would be nice.

Hands Made for Weaving, with Nails Sharp as Claws

T HE BLUE HOUSE BESIDE THE BIG SALT KEPT ITS SECRETS, AS DID THE world weaver who lived there. It stood on the crest of a bluff, overlooking the sea, its clapboards blasted by saltwater thunderstorms and scorched by sun. Its porch held two ironwork rocking chairs, worn to comfort, but only one had ever been used at a time. And that was by the current weaver in residence who, on top of everything else she did, was responsible for tending the veil between worlds. For years, no one disturbed their companionable silence, enhanced only by the lapping of waves along the shore.

When Mami Wata sent her hurry-canes, the world weaver would put on her linseed-oil-cured cape, secure the door to the house, protect it with powdered brick, and head out in the driving rain to look for mermaids.

Most times, there was only one, hidden in the arching sand dunes, cowering from her mother's wrath. Goddesses never looked kindly on a lack of good sense, and getting caught on land at low tide was the height of foolishness. The weaver would speak to the maids in whispers that they heard over the wind and thrashing waters, coaxing them back to the ocean's embrace. She guided them as they crawled, hand over hand, tails steering, bald heads sleek and glistening, into the waves. After they disappeared, the storm would slowly die, and the turbulent waters would return to their gentle, cat-like lapping.

Far fewer were the maids dragged ashore in nets by fishermen, who quickly became entranced by their not-quite-humanness. Some had single tails like fish or sea ponies, others had eight or more trailing tentacles, coiling around the rough netting enclosing them. When that happened, the world weaver would discover the fishermen poking and prodding the maids instead of finding shelter from the sea goddess's wrath. It took some doing to convince the men to let Mami Wata's gals go, but the world weaver mostly managed it without bloodshed.

Only once had she fought a man. He was a fisher who'd thought he'd be able to feast for weeks on the thick, heavy mermaid tail. After, she lifted the tortured child from the bottom of the bloodstained shad boat, dressed her wounds, and carried her back to her mother. The boat, she burned for kindling.

It had been many a year since she had to leave her home and search the shores, and she found herself restless, unable to find comfort in her four walls. The house sighed, understanding, but not wanting her to go. It felt secure with her presence and her protection. Without her, someone else might paint its wooden slats white or yellow instead of the blue that kept the haints away.

The house wasn't actually afraid of being haunted, but it liked living beings inside itself, and from what it experienced over the years, the living and the dead rarely got along.

It had been many a year since the world weaver had stitched together the veil. When she was younger and still had dreams of living among the masses, she'd been on call for such repairs. But she soon found that despite her ability to patch rips between the worlds, usually caused by careless fools without respect for or belief in magic, no one wanted her around. She was an all too visible reminder that, while diminished, magic still lived and breathed on the human side of the veil.

So the world weaver had packed her splinter needles and her frog-hair thread and left the city and her dreams of living among others behind. The creatures from the breach that still survived followed her to the blue house where she tore a hole in the world with her fingernails to allow them to return home. Then she sat on a sand dune, tucked her skirt between her thighs, and whipstitched the hole closed again.

The wind picked up, blowing her tears across her bronze cheeks. She didn't brush them away but turned into the wind's force, allowing it to take her breath as well. Gasping, she sucked in a deep lungful of sea air, and it calmed her enough to return to the cozy warmth of the house.

Never had the house understood her desire for solitude, but it accepted this need with the grace of its years. When it was younger and newly built, it might have kicked up a fuss, made a key stick in its lock or kept the fire from sparking. But age after age housing world weavers had taught it that each weaver must come to terms with herself eventually.

It was at times like this when she was grateful for her position. Nowhere was the barrier between worlds thinner than at the sea's edge. The ocean didn't need a tear or a rip, it seemed, to bring the beautifully strange into this world. On her daily walk down the wooden pathway to the beach, she and the house had seen wondrous beings and marveled. The pair had helped many return home, even buried those that refused succor.

A few times, the odd visitor managed to wiggle through the veil between worlds without her notice—she was still a tad human and therefore not perfect. All weavers retained a breath of humanity, which made them a little patient with the more trying aspects of it. Those wondrous creatures that didn't die in the cities were captured and tortured for research. Word got around that this was the fate of the uncanny and most stopped trying to visit.

One clear morning, during her walk along the sands, she saw someone scurrying away with a small bundle. She shouted after them, but they didn't turn and outdistanced her quickly, tucking the cloth-wrapped package under their arm. City folk, she thought. Someone who had overfished their permit, or didn't have one, taking more food than they needed or could reasonably sell.

She made her way back to the blue house and sat on its porch in one of the ironwork rockers, to drink a cup of peach tea that was really wine. Her bones ached and the back of her neck prickled where the tight coils of her hair managed to escape her brush. Clouds amassed in the previously clear sky faster than winds could carry them.

At that moment, she knew what the person had done.

"Mami Wata wants her baby back, House." But she didn't move, choosing instead to rock herself slowly, soothing her anxiety at the gathering storm. For once, she wanted to be the one someone came home to after the work was done. She wanted to wait with the house, keeping herself warm with tea that was wine, and waiting, watching the dunes for her loved one's return.

The house's floorboards creaked in acknowledgement. It also knew what those clouds meant: that the world weaver was going away.

Winds whipped up fierce, bringing sand and grit up on the porch to batter at the woman's face.

She groaned but rose from the rocker, grit crunching under her feet. Mami Wata didn't like waiting, and her storm was something to behold. Sand rose in whorls above the seagrass, tiny funnel tempests. The house's windows rattled, and its moans tore at her heart.

"You win," she muttered.

Outside, the world weaver nailed up thin squares of wood to cover the house's windows, and tacked up sheets of tincloth to the inside windows in case anything penetrated the glass. The house rasped, its floorboards squeaking against each other. She didn't go upstairs to cover the top windows, choosing instead to let the house see down into the city from its perch on the sea's edge, hoping that would lessen its worry.

"I know," she soothed. "I know. I won't be gone long."

She had no idea how long she'd be gone or if she'd be able to return. In her experience, and in the writings of weavers before her, those that stole the children of the sea would kill to retain their ill-gotten prize. She wasn't immortal, she knew that, but what would kill her? That was a mystery.

Once the world weaver had packed a small bag with a woven blanket, a skin of seawater, and a few strips of dried fish from her own food supply, she donned her linseed-oil-cured cape, secured the door, and protected it. She headed across the sand toward town, the wind and rain at her back, the goddess's whisper in her ear.

She worried she had forgotten the way, but her recollection of the paths was still sharp, possibly because the memory of the way the city folk treated her was also stingingly fresh in her mind. On she walked, sipping from her skin of seawater, until sand became dirt and dirt became stone.

Having lived for so long on the sea, alone with just the house, the city felt tight— the buildings too tall, too close. Her steps quickened in hopes of finding the baby soon and returning home.

She rarely thought of the house as home, but it was. The blue clapboard, always visible through fog and ocean mist, warmed her, cheered her. She wasn't sure she had ever told it that, but she vowed to the moment she returned. Nothing that meant so much should feel unappreciated.

The gazes of the townsfolk lay heavy on her as she walked the cobbled streets, the stones paining her booted feet. The storm hadn't followed her to the city, but she sensed it there, just outside the town, watching and waiting to strike. Hold on, she thought. Can't go charging in all the time. Even goddesses, especially nervous mothers, needed reminding at times.

This town wasn't the same as the one she'd left. The symbols the townsfolk had painted on their doors and shop signs to prevent magic were gone. Even the shops themselves had changed. No meat hung in windows, no freshly-dug vegetables in trays outside, ready to be scrubbed and eaten. No longer did scents of baking bread and cakes dance in the air. Gone was the excited bartering and the clip-schlop of hooved animals. Instead, the sounds were piercing shrieks and wails, and they frightened her heart into a flutter. This was not the world she had left, the world she had so wanted to be a part of—the one that had driven her away.

Even the folk had changed. She didn't mind the different clothes and hair—those styles never stayed long. It was their reaction to her presence. Once, they'd have avoided her, crossing the street to not have her steps cross theirs. Now, they followed her at a distance, pointing fingers and little boxes at her, and laughing behind their hands. Unsettled by their attention, she wondered how long she'd sat alone in the blue house overlooking the sea.

This town was new and unfamiliar, but yet again, the folk here had judged her as apart from them. She did not understand their speech, but at least she could make sense of the signs and maps with some effort.

How was she supposed to find the baby among all this? Even the feel of magic had left this place. She kept walking the stone, resolute in her task, sand crunching beneath her.

Sand.

A sprinkling of golden powder lay between the cobbled stones on the road, winding down the street, then up onto the footpath in front of the row of glass-fronted shops, only to disappear around a corner. She followed the glimmer like crushed gold, heedless of the curiosity behind her.

The trail led to a building more like those she remembered, long and narrow, and fronted by a line of four doors, likely an old stable. Someone had finally noticed the trail of grit and had tried to sweep it away. But the wind had swirled the sand back into a pile outside one of the doors, of which the top half was open, and after glancing around, the weaver approached and peered in.

Darkness filled the space, save for a flameless lamp crouching in a shadowed corner of the hay-scented stable. She pulled the handle grip; the bottom of the door swung open without a sound and she carefully closed it behind her. She crept in, letting her eyes adjust to the wan light filtering through the wooden slats. The storm held off for now, but the weaver knew she had to be quick. Mami missed her girl, and there was no telling what she would do in her worry.

Riffling through the dusty shelves, she found papers marking sales of goods— old magic, roots and herbs and oils of bark, mostly for gentle spells to calm the mind and soul. As she read more, the receipts showed contents of darker charms—to hex a family line or harden the heart against a former lover, to end a life. At the end of it all, a paper with one item listed:

SOLD—ONE SEA MONSTER

(Cannot guarantee living, but care will be taken to assure arrival in one piece. Good for weather spells or as a curio for the morbid.)

The world weaver threw down the papers, tore open the drawers and cabinets, looking for the child. In her haste, she forgot to be quiet. The moment she drew open a hatch and saw the crab child lying on a tattered cloth was the moment a shadow fell over her shoulder. She turned, and saw a figure looming over her. Then she saw the pipe—metal, rusty, heavy-looking.

He brought it whistling down on the top of her head.

A splash, like a boulder falling into the ocean, sounded as the pipe connected with her skull and continued on through to slam against the dirt floor. The blow jarred the thief's shoulder and he gave a brief cry. The pipe clattered to the dirt floor. Nonplussed, the weaver blinked, then wiped off a sprinkle of rust that had fallen on her nose.

"Unwise," she said, grabbing the man by his collar. She dragged him to the far wall of the barn, then clawed a long, jagged rip in the veil. "Show me horrors," she told the opening before shoving the man's head through. He writhed and jerked, but if he screamed, it was lost to the veil.

The crab child giggled and clicked its claws.

When flickers and snaps of light appeared in her sightline, she turned to see the city folk with their slim black boxes pointed at her, flashing lights erupting from them.

"You stood there!" she shouted. "You all stood there and watched him strike me!"

The world weaver then grabbed the child, wrapped it in the blanket and pushed through the folk in her way. She did not stop walking, heedless of their calls to her asking for what sounded like *'picts*. At least now they were afraid to touch her. The child gurgled and rooted at her breast, but she gave it a strip of dried fish, which it suckled at happily.

In the distance, the clouds were retreating, almost as if they were pulling her back to the sea, and when she saw the house still standing against the violence of the storm, she smiled. As she got closer, she saw a dark-skinned woman sitting on the porch, plucking shells from her halo of coral-colored hair before twining it into plaits.

"Weaver," the woman said, flicking the waterfall of braids over her shoulder. She straightened the hem of her dress, iridescent with rainbows.

"Mami Wata," she answered, then recalled her vow. "I'm glad to be home to you, House."

Under her feet, the floorboards creaked in welcome.

"May I?" the goddess asked, opening her arms. The crab child went to her, and she cuddled it close, whispering song in its shell-like ear. "I have yet to thank you for your help all these years, Weaver. I have been remiss."

It was best to say nothing in these circumstances, and the world weaver took this option.

"What would you request of me?" The goddess turned her grey-green eyes, set deep into her dark skin, on the weaver. She rocked the chair gently, soothing the child.

The house creaked a warning. It saw the city folk coming, determination rising from them.

More than anything, the world weaver wanted her solitude back, and she knew these folk would not allow her to have it. No, solitude was not what she wished for. It was peace. Eternal peace and the company of one who has loved and cared for her. She looked up at the house, her home, her love.

"I am pleased with your choice. Do you agree, House?"

A squeak of floorboards sounded its agreement.

The weaver turned to the goddess. Waves rose up, crashed against the shore. Thunder boomed, while a flash of lighting took her vision for a brief moment. When her vision returned, the house was gone, the rockers now on the sand. Mami Wata sat as she had before her display, smirk showing she was pleased with her work. Next to her sat a man, his lapis-hued face weathered, but kind. Smile tentative, he rose from the rocker and approached her.

"I didn't think you'd mind if I kept the blue," he said.

"I . . . I don't mind at all," she whispered as he slipped his roughened hand into hers.

Mami Wata stood, clutching the crab child to her. "I've made a home for you, near mine, of course. I shall still need help with my brood."

She sauntered away toward the ocean, her dress clinging closer to her body, until it was impossible to tell it from skin. When she dove into the waves, her tail surfaced for a moment, wide as a whale's, then the goddess and her child were gone.

The weaver stared for a few moments, gently squeezing House's hand.

"Are you happy, House?"

"I've been happy with you for eons," he said.

Hand in hand they walked along the sand, following in the goddess's footsteps and into the playful sea, the excited cries of Mami Wata's girls welcoming them home.

Shine, Blackberry Wine

I SAT ON MY BEST FRIEND'S BEIGE TWILL SOFA, SULFUR-RICH MARSH BREEZE blowing in through the wide-open windows, mixing with the metallic scent of her homemade moonshine. Distant ocean waves, with their rhythmic Zen-like lapping, gave me a serenity the mewling seagulls didn't. I licked the sheen of sweat from my upper lip and asked her again.

"You promise you won't tell anyone? Swear?"

Keira nodded. "I swear, damn. When, in all the years I've known you, have I ever told anyone anything you said not to?"

"Never, but—" I shrugged, tugging at the backside of my shorts where they stuck to my thighs. "Why the hell won't you get air conditioning? It's hotter than Satan's bathwater in here. You do know this is Charleston?"

"My place is on Wadmalaw, actually." Heat never seemed to bother Keira. Even now, while I was sweating like a derby winner, she looked cool and relaxed; her thick, twisted locs hanging over her shoulder and down her back to her elbows. She took a sip from her glass of shine, not wincing at the sharp taste. "And you know why. This used to be enslaved housing and it's protected property. There's only so many changes I can make." It was her turn to shrug . "Not sure I want to modernize it too much, anyway."

"Ugh." I took another sip from my icy glass, the only chilled thing in the room besides Keira, and flopped back on the sofa. She always made the best drinks, crafted from her own home-distilled spirits. This one was somewhere between backyard moonshine and bathtub gin, enhanced with the woody, fresh zing of juniper.

"Just tell me what it is that you came running over here for so quick-like." Keira stretched her feet out in front of her; they were bare and a polished walnut not unlike the hardwood floor beneath them. She picked at a flaking piece of red polish on her pinky toe.

But it hadn't been quick-like. For over almost two weeks now, I'd been having strange dreams. Dreams had always been a part of my life growing up—my grandmother, an Afro-Choctaw, used to interpret mine when I was a little girl. But these hadn't been the normal dreams I'd had as a child. I wasn't being chased or falling or spitting all of my teeth into my palm. These were—

"Hello, Randie?" She waved her hand in front of my face. "Planet Earth is calling. Return to us. Come in, space cadet."

Keira's sarcasm was strong enough to pull me out of my reverie. "Oh, right. Sorry. Promise me you'll listen. Just . . . don't say anything until I'm finished, okay?"

She'd been about to say something snarky when she stopped and looked deeply into my eyes. Whatever she saw there made her nod. "Okay. Promise."

"There was a key," I said. "in the first dream. It started with that."

A strange key waits on the dining room table. It's the length of my palm, but lightweight, almost floaty. When I look at it closely, there's a pattern of engraved vines on the key's head and it makes a sort of dense curtain. It feels damp, but my hand stays dry when I touch it.

Then I feel someone's stare heavy on me and I glance up. It's a woman—at least, I think it's a woman because I remember looking at her lipstick. It makes her lips look like they're pale green blushed with rose. She smiles, then all of a sudden, there's . . . I don't know . . . a flash of some kind and I'm on a winding stone path. There's a city in the distance, glittering with this haunting, almost aqueous glow.

The scene flashes again to show me algae-covered columns, then statues of these fish-like people. Quick pictures, like a speeded up film montage, you know? Then full screen zoom in on this coral gate. I put the key in the lock and it opens.

I drain the rest of my moonshine, ice clinking against the tumbler, as Keira watches me, silent. For a few moments, she doesn't say or do anything. The sun has started its descent, and I wonder how long I've been talking lost in this memory, because the air hasn't cooled off at all.

"When I wake up from these dreams, my body is wet with sweat, but I'm not hot. Every morning, I have these faint red circles on my face and chest that I have to cover with makeup. I'm just exhausted. I have to cover the circles under my eyes as well."

"Dreams?" Keira asked, emphasis on the s. "So, how many are we talking here?"

"At least one a night for about . . . well, almost two weeks. These past few nights though, it's like I've actually been doing things inside my dream. You know, I'm working all day at the school, then moving around through the dream all night. I fall asleep easily, but I'm not rested." I picked up my glass and put to my lips, but realize it's empty and instead roll it between my palms. "Dreams are supposed to be manifestations of the subconscious mind. What is it that I'm not resolving during my waking hours?"

Keira eased herself up, padded over to her adjoining kitchen and took two wine glasses from the cabinet, holding them upside down by their stems between her fingers. She pulled a dark green bottle from the wine rack, then returned to her seat next me. After breaking the wax seal, she filled both glasses halfway, leaving the bottle open to the coming night air.

I touch my glass to hers and we both sip. The taste of this wine brings me back to my childhood: running around at the edge of the woods with Keira, stealing sun-warmed blackberries, heedless of whose property line we crossed. Those sweet berry vines pricked our fingers, and we sucked in tiny drops of our blood with their dark juice.

"Do you think it's because I moved away from here?" I asked. "The unresolved issues, I mean. There was so much mom and dad expected from me . . . I just couldn't take it. Work and church and looking after gran while they went off to prayer meetings." The memory of it weighed on me even now, stooping my shoulders.

I didn't have . . . I couldn't do what I wanted—my family wouldn't let me. They had plans. So I left home right after graduation. But I was back now. I should have laughed at how ridiculous this all was. I was back home five years later, with debt up to my eyeballs and a twice-broken heart.

Keira's smooth, dark locs sway as she shakes her head. "Naw, I don't think so. But only you can answer that."

Nodding, I continued recanting my dream. "Anyway, the next time I fall asleep, I see the key again. Except this time, the picture—that network of vines on the key's head—is open and there's an image of the gate to the stone city. That . . . that means something, right?"

She opened her mouth to speak, but I held up a finger, asking her to wait. I had to get this out; the feel of these images in my mind pressed deeper, rooting into my every waking moment.

In a flash, I'm back in the city, but it looks deserted. I know it isn't, though. I feel it. As I walk through the streets, there's this eerie sound, like when you sit at the bottom of a pool. I try to catch any sign of movement, but there's none. Instead, I see an obelisk in the middle of the city, all these unknown symbols carved into one side of the rock. So I go over and study it, but I have no idea what any of it means.

I fold my legs under me and sit back, pressing my shoulders into the cushions. The wine is slowly relaxing me and I rush the next part of the story.

"But I'm determined to figure it out. I touch the rock all over. Nothing. By this time, I'm upset, frustrated. I go to walk away, trailing my hand over the face of the stone and it warms under my palm, turning into full glow, like the beam from a lighthouse. There's a silhouette in the distance.

This time, I think it's a man. He comes closer to me and with each step, I think I know him, but I'm not sure. I almost have it, then it's gone. He embraces me, then his fingers are in my hair, loosening my braids, which then turn into . . . these tentacles. I shake my head and it feels so good for them to be free. I stretch them out and they reach so far . . .

He lowers me to the bed and I slide my leg over his, situating my body upright on top of his prone one. And it's like . . . I'm riding him. But I'm also . . . I'm looking at us together on the bed as well. I hear this sloshing of water as we do it. And I'm panting and he's pumping and I know it's us churning this water into a thick maelstrom.

My tentacled hair is waving around wildly, growing longer and thicker, then the stalks shoot upward, out of the dream and into . . . like . . . real life. I grab something, someone, with the tentacles.

I can smell it almost, taste it. She's trembling, petrified. A whimper. She twists onto her back and tries to kick free, but I'm too strong. Then she screams. It sounds like nothing to me, so I cut off her terrified wail with the dripping slap of another limb across her mouth. Suckers constrict around her jaw until I hear a resounding crunch.

I tighten my grip on her and I . . .

Tear her apart.

I sighed and sat back, worn from recanting the story. The sleepless nights had begun to catch up with me, and I sipped the sweet-tart blackberry wine as I pressed my aching shoulders back into the sofa.

"Wow," Keira breathed, her eyes wide. She hugged me, surrounding me in her earthy green scent. "It's gonna be okay, girl. Don't worry."

"I'm not going crazy, am I?" I asked, shaking my head. "This is so surreal. I can't wrap my head around it."

"You're not going crazy." She lifted the mass of heavy locs from her neck and tossed them over her shoulder. A circular stick and poke tattoo—maybe a snake or an eel—graced the flesh behind her ear.

I frowned. "When did you get that? I've never seen—"

"They're the ones who gonna lose they minds, Randie."

I dragged my gaze back to her, searching her face for some sign that I'd heard her incorrectly. Her eyes were clear and alert, focused on me. "What d'you mean by *they*?"

She ignored my question, instead leaning over to light the trio of candles on her coffee table.

"Keira?" I asked, confusion evident in my voice. "What—"

"All of them," she said finally. "Those who doubt us and our power."

"Who is us?" I was frightened now. The candlelight was making unnatural shadows on my best friend's face, putting her dark skin into even deeper shadow.

"Your mama didn't think you'd be the one to get visions of the coming, but I knew." Her self-satisfied chuckle followed her as she got up from the couch and pulled an old leather-bound book from a shelf. "I always know."

I tried to get up, but my limbs were heavy, weighted. The urge to weep welled up in me, and I no longer had the strength to hold back the tears. I couldn't turn my head, but I could hear Keira moving around her tiny house on the marsh, humming to herself songs I recalled from my childhood.

"You know," she said, "It's probably because you spent all those years away that it took so long for you to see. What did he look like?" Her usually modulated voice pitched up a level with her excitement. "No, no, don't tell me. We'll know soon enough."

From the candles, a deep scent rose, one of moss and smoke and steel. When Keira returned into my line of sight, she was holding another pillar candle, running a wicked knife back and forth through the flickering orange flame. I whimpered, and she leaned close to brush my hair from my forehead, bringing the heated metal within a blink of my eye.

"Shhh," she murmured, kissing my temple. Footsteps skittered outside on the worn, wooden planks leading through the salt marsh to my best friend's door. She pressed the warm blade against my skin, then hers, letting the drops form a network of swirling vines.

Flickers of light catch my swimming vision. In the encroaching darkness, amongst the cicada song, giddy flames dart through the surrounding marsh. No . . . not dart. Travel. What my mind knows are exploding marsh gasses—incendiary moments only—arrange themselves into a distinct pattern. A line that coils through the waving sea grasses, filing toward the cabin.

"K-kay," I managed through the paralysis invading my body, but she placed her cool fingertips against my lips and they managed no more.

"Before the rest of the Order gets here," Keira said, hugging my stiff body. "I just wanna say I'm so glad you came back. Proud of you, girl."

Miss Beulah's Braiding and Life Change Salon

T HE CHIME ABOVE MY SHOP DOOR RINGS.

It heralds a young woman wearing a head wrap boasting a network of silvery constellations on indigo, interspersed with the occasional yellow-gold moon. The wrap itself is made of silk—not the finest grade, mind you, but sufficient to conceal what she must see as a fault. None of her hair is visible, but the contorted celestial bodies show the fabric is at the end of its tether.

Her gaze flicks around, lighting on every little thing in my salon, then leaping away to the next. From the incense cone on the windowsill emitting apple and lily-scented curls of smoke, to the crisp, white sailcloth curtains snapping sharp in front of the open window. Then to the merry fire burning in the iron stove across from me that consumes all it is fed without giving off heat. Finally, her weary, heavy-lidded eyes settle on me.

I do not get up—we djinn do not like to move much, especially while in our solid forms—but I smile and motion to the styling chair in front of me. She stares at me for a short while, and while she does, I can hear her mind clicking like some clockwork toy, trying to make sense of what she sees. Her eyes get wider as they take me in, lightening the dark rings under them for a moment.

But she doesn't run. She doesn't scream. A good sign for a first-time client. After a deep breath, she walks with birdlike steps from the front door across the gleaming tiles and sits in my chair. She removes her head wrap with care, releasing her hair from its prison before folding the cloth into thirds and picking at a stray thread. Her gaze stays firmly in her lap.

And I know her struggle.

This poor thing takes a lot of time to try and keep this head of hair, but it resists her most valiant efforts. Every strand, every coil, is a blessing and a curse. Each lock must be cared for tenderly, not touched by brush, but eased apart with the wide teeth of an oil-soaked wooden comb and the caress of pomade-laced fingers, searching out each tangle and coaxing it free.

"What you getting today?" While I have an idea what she wants, I always ask. New clients tend to be nervous and get more wary when I seem to know too much. And even I am not right all of the time.

"I lost my job, Miss Beulah." Her voice is a whisper of shame and her head tries to dip lower. But I lift it gently with my fingers under her chin.

"That ain't always a bad thing, you know, doll." I can never remember all of their names. Don't even ask anymore. I used to try, thinking it made them feel better, but I realized they don't much care what I call them. I know how to do their hair, I know how to design their dreams, and that is enough.

She chokes back sobs, swallows hard before speaking. "I can't make it without a job. It's not just me, I have a son—"

"You want it back or you want another job?" Any soul can see that isn't her real trouble. Her pain is larger, deeper, born of powerlessness and fear. It is a pain that doesn't leave, even in the midst of sleep, what little of it she is getting lately. Sad to say, if the return of her job is all she can ask for, then that is all I can give her. I am bound by the laws of my people as much as she is by hers.

She takes a while to think about this, and I run my fingers over and through her hair, massaging her scalp and her neck and shoulders until she slumps back in my chair.

"Whatever you think is best." She sighs.

Her hair, a coarse, dusty brown, is dry and thinning, but her scalp is clean, free of dandruff and residue. She did what I asked and washed her hair before she came. The sharp scents of peppermint and sulfur cling to it and I wrinkle my nose.

As my fingers tumble through her tresses, I see she had worked hard at that job, tried to be what they wanted, but she had been fighting a losing battle. They had other plans from the start, and she was filling a space until they found the one they really wanted. But I also see the reason for her appointment. When I work the tangles from her coils, I smooth her hair back from her high forehead. It barely reaches her chin. Her ends are even, clipped neat.

"You cut it?" It comes out sharp, an accusation, and she responds as such.

"The other woman who was doing my hair said it needed a trim." Her voice is defensive, a shield against further hurt. "Split, raggedy ends and all. Even some of the videos online say to get your ends trimmed to help it grow."

Glad she can't see my mouth as it twists, I return the soothing tone to my voice. "And it work for you?"

"No, not really."

"Well, you here now." I turn the swivel chair to the mirror. "Gonna be all right."

Her eyes hold nervousness, flickers of fear, and a fragile hope. Under my fingers, her scalp feels feverish, damp. I smile to reassure her.

"You need to choose," I say. "If you keep this style, you get your job back, but no more. All will go back to like before. That what you want?" *Ask me, chile. That is the only way to get what you truly want. A little of it, anyway.*

She trembles under my stroking fingers. "No," she murmurs, only just louder than the crackle of the fire. Soon, I see tears on her cheeks, her neck. I feel their heat as they tumble, slide, drip from her chin onto the fabric cape I fastened around her neck.

"Then what?" I speak soft, tender, like to a fearful creature. And that she is. "You told me what happen to you, not what you want."

She heaves the words through thickened breathing. "I want . . ." Deep gulps of incense-laced air. Finally, she speaks again. "I don't want her to go. Not yet. I just need . . ." She swallows, picks at the faded violet varnish on her thumbnail. "A little more time."

Her watery brown eyes meet all of mine in the mirror for a moment, then she becomes more interested in the stitching on her decent enough pocketbook.

"With your ma?" I prompt.

"Yes, ma'am. Just 'til Travis grows up."

I look at her face, narrow determined chin, old soul eyes open wide. Her tremors ebb away until she is only listing slightly from side to side in the chair. Rocking herself to a calm.

"Okay," I tell her, rat-tail comb in one hand, wide-toothed comb in another. "Let us make a change." In another pair of hands, I take a jar of fluffy cream, my own blend—rich with seed oils and honey from bees drunk on shea tree pollen.

While I open the jar, I pat her shoulder. "You look nervous, chile."

We are the only ones in the shop, as I never book more than one client at a time, even though I have multiples of everything—chairs, shampoo bowls, arms, hands . . .

"I've never had a . . . well, you know." She doesn't meet my eyes in the mirror this time and I suppress my chuckle.

"No, suppose not." I appreciate her sensitivity in not calling me a genie. A captor's term. I am the only jiniri —female djinn —in the Southeast with a beauty shop. For all I know, maybe even the entire country. Since the law freeing us was passed, many hide, especially those of us that look different. But I have chosen not to. What was once taken—my wishes—I now sell, for my benefit and for theirs.

With care, I part a section of her hair and clip the rest of it away while I apply my scented balm to her strands. They soak the nourishment up, and plump from their drink, bend easily. I twist, then braid, winding it into a rope-like plait.

"Want a magazine?" Two, three sections at a time—part, apply, braid, pin— now that she has voiced her desires.

She tries to shake her head, but my fingers tighten against her scalp and she winces. "No, I want to watch you work."

I work on her for two hours, twisting and molding her hair into something new. Spirals and constellations on indigo. Once or twice, she almost falls asleep, but her forward movement wakes her. Each time, there is a second of fear in her eyes when she sees me looming over her. Six hands moving like dervishes through her hair and scalp. I am not offended. The third time, I ease her head back onto the neck rest of my chair and sleep spirits her away. She snores softly, with a light wheeze.

Trilling music sounds, muffled, distant. She stirs, sits up. Fumbles in her bag and puts a phone to her ear. I pretend to only hear one side of the conversation. "This is Teena . . . Yes? She is? Oh, thank God . . . No, no. I'll be there. Thank you. Bye."

My work on her hair is finished before she replaces the phone.

"Good news?"

Teena nods. Our gazes lock again and she gives me a hesitant, shaky smile. It is a start.

"All done." I pat her shoulder.

Finally, she sees—really sees—her crown of glory. "Oh my God."

She breathes the words as she touches the once-dusty hair, now darkened with moisture and healed with oil, with reverent fingers. The braids and twists glisten where they lay in intricate patterns against her fine head.

"This doesn't even look like me." She shoves the scarf into her pocketbook.

"Like it?" I recap the jar of balm, remove the crisp puffs of shed hair from both combs and throw them into the fire that constantly burns in my shop.

"I love it." Teena pauses, clutches the bag to her chest. "H-h-have you taken your payment?"

"I have, thank you."

Yes, I have eaten her nightmares. They were denser, richer than most I have tasted. Ones where she was being chased, where she was falling unceasingly, screaming into an indifferent night were deep with salty, meaty savor. The one where she was drowning, sweet and light as foam. After only a small portion, I was replete.

She nods and gets up from my chair. Anxious sweat has dampened her skirt until it clings to the backs of her thighs. She tugs it free. "I guess I'm all set, then."

"Yes."

Teena chews her lip then stops as if she'd had a lifetime of scolding about the habit. "How long will this last?"

I take pity on her and answer the question not asked. "If your ma starts feeling poorly again, make an appointment." My eyes narrow at her, five slits of sharp focus, to ensure she is listening. "But you cannot wear this style forever. A time will come when you must accept that."

At the door, she pauses, turns to look at me. Straight in the face this time with no dread or panic. "What do I say if someone asks me about my hair? About you?"

I am so full. My eyes grow heavy. I let them all close, one by one by one by one. "You tell them Miss Beulah does your hair."

The chime above the door rings, letting me know she has left. I reach over and flip the switch that locks the front door. I have time for a nap before my next client. Time to weave my own dreams.

I yawn.

Plenty of time.

Stages of the Witch

SEER: YOU'RE ABLE TO TELL THE EXACT POINT WHEN HE'S LOST INTEREST. In you. In everything. You notice his gaze on his plate, the restaurant, the door, everywhere else. You watch him slip away, as if through your fingers, into a place beyond far. Beyond the veil. Beyond you.

Empath: You feel his distance as though it were a gut punch. Or a knife wound, saber-deep and gaping. No, you feel it as a paper cut—no sound, no source that you can tell, only a stinging flinch before the flare of pain. Soon your paper cut wells with blood. You lick it off and taste dirty metal along with your carefully applied hand cream, its flavor like dying roses.

Potion-Maker: You try to alleviate the pain. At first, you are careful— measure, mix, select the right container. Then you sip your concoction, sip until your choices don't matter. The taste is at first sweet, then sharp, like your memories. You drink it down, not realizing you've made a sleep potion. Or was it one of forgetfulness?

Telepath: It wasn't forgetfulness. When you wake, your mind calls out, the words a primal scream into the void of your soul. Why him? Why you? Why this? All is quiet for endless heartbeats, then a voice responds.

Scryer: You search, sending out your tentacles, testing to find that voice. It's near, you know. But the map you have is ancient—a few moments old. You refresh the page and the map changes again. A red dot pulses, hovers. Suddenly, you're not alone and

Everything

has

changed.

 You have joined a **Coven**. Become its third.

The first teaches you her craft while anointing you with words. *Better. Try. Rise up. Fight.* The hex is sand in your mouth, and you spit it out, unable to believe its power.

Again, she says.

Again.

Again.

Soon, the spell runs like sun-warmed nectar from your tongue, **Spellcaster**, and your lips move quick as frightened moths.

The second lurks at the edge of your lessons, silent and watchful as she lights candles dressed with Roman chamomile and verbena. A mote of dust floats in the air above you as she dives into your subconscious. There, she explores until she finds the rip. Where your true self has torn away from the world-weary one, shrinking under the clinging vines of the world's words.

Unloveable.

Unwanted.

Not enough . . .

Instead of snipping off these vines, she coats them with honeyed words, and they become pliant like thread. Thread she uses to stitch your selves back together.

Embrace this twoness, **Shadowworker**, *she croons. You are woman and witch, light and dark, novice and sage. You are in this world but not of it.*

When she emerges, she collapses to the floor between you and the first. While her smile is tired, it is triumphant.

There is a tender place inside you, a soreness, that feels purged clean.

You are enough of a seer to tell, and enough of an empath to know

You are **Enough**.

Don't You Weep

God gave Noah the rainbow sign
No more water, the fire next time.
—Negro spiritual

I T WAS 4:45 A.M., AND THE DEATH CHAMBER WAS EMPTY.
Corrections Officer Tonia Davis didn't start her shift until 6:00, but as
she skirted past the viewing area that looked into the narrow room where
the state's hundred-year-old electric chair stood, a cold chill ran through her
sturdy back. She hated coming this way. A glance at the chair, crouched there
like some archaic, wooden creature, waiting to receive its sacrifice, made her
ill. Even though the executions the state held now were via lethal injection, the
fact this monstrosity served as an eager backup disturbed her more than she
wanted to admit.

Executions in the state had restarted this year after a twenty-year hiatus
and two failed popular referendums, and already, Tonia was reconsidering her
choice of career. Four years in the military stateside hadn't prepared her for this.
She shuffled to the guard breakroom to finish her breakfast and claim a little
peace before the start of the workday.

Especially since another execution was scheduled for the end of the week.

Tonia gulped the rest of her vanilla-syrup-laced drink. There was only enough coffee in it to give it the appropriate hue; the drink itself was more milkshake than caffeine. She told herself she needed the sweet. It helped offset the bitterness brewing all around her. Inside her too if she was honest.

"You in early. Drinkin that sugar water."

"Mine ya business, Ferrar."

From the talk round the facility, Ferrar had been minding everybody's business but his own the entirety of the time he'd been working here—almost ten years. He'd been riding that reception desk just as long. Everybody knew he wanted to be on patrol, swaggering his little self down the hallways and telling people they were getting exactly what was coming to them. Even Tonia, who'd recently had her second anniversary of employment at the women's correctional facility, knew, but she wasn't going to tell him he needed to do his current job before management would put him up for another one.

He looked her up and down with more judgement than desire and took a long sip of the inky swill that passed for coffee in the guard's breakroom. "Hmph. You must love this place 'cause you stay getting here early."

Tonia sucked her teeth. "It's called working. Try it sometime."

"I do zactly what I need to do round here."

Yeah, Tonia thought. *Keep telling yourself that.*

Tonia tapped the edge of the paper cup on the table, tilted her head back, and let the cap of sweetened foam slide down into her mouth. "I don't have time to fool with you, Ferrar. Have a good day."

She tossed the cup in the trash and strode down to the prisoner's ward for her morning ritual, nodding to another officer passing in the hall. It didn't matter that Ferrar knew what she was doing coming in early lately. Everyone knew everyone's business in this prison. It was like its own small town within a town, where it was hard to keep secrets or find privacy unless people made a special effort to turn their backs.

Like they had with her morning ritual.

Every day for the past two weeks, Tonia had been trying to guess what Lula Mae Heyward would choose for her last meal.

Despite the heat of summer outside, the prisoner cells remained chilly. The stone floor that could be hosed clean, the iron bars—hell, the concrete walls themselves—all conspired to retain the cold and to fuel the misery that spawned here.

"Mornin', ladies."

Her greeting was met mostly with silence, save for mumbled, incomprehensible groans and a few enthusiastic curses. There was no trouble first thing in the morning because the other inmates knew the schedule as well as she did. Sunrise on Saturday morning would be the last one Ms. Lula would ever see. A hush, an unnatural blanketing of sound, grew over this wing of the prison. A skittish waiting, like an animal hiding until the predator has passed.

Tonia reached the last cell on the left, leaned her side against the heat-stealing concrete. Without a greeting, she asked the questions she'd prepared after searching through several classic cooking websites.

"Lobster thermidor?"

"Nope."

"Oysters?"

"Nah-ah."

"Fillet mignon?"

"Wrong again, Officer." Lula Mae leaned back on the threadbare cot in the eight-by-eight cell that had been her home for the past twenty-one years. The bedframe creaked, and the elderly woman, deftly for her age, avoided the exposed spring that poked out of the graying mattress stuffing. She was spry for what Tonia had discovered from her file was her eightieth year.

"I said you can call me Tonia."

"You got a title, betta let people use it." Lula Mae chuckled and shifted on her cot, the springs twanging under the thin mattress. Her oaky complexion was barely lined, despite her advanced age and the circumstances of her incarceration. Her face and neck were littered with pinhead-sized moles. Her laugh was husky, rusty, and harsh as a winter cough.

Tonia smiled. A tired one, a bitter one, maybe . . . but a smile all the same. "Well, how about—"

"Uh uh. That's your three tries for the day."

"Well, I've got three more nights to guess. I'll get it. Oh . . ." Tonia leaned against the bars of the cell enclosing the state's oldest female inmate and, though she hated to admit it, her closest confidant. "I'm sorry, Miz Heyward."

"What for? It's the truth, ain't it?" She shrugged her narrow shoulders, cloaked in a fading pink cardigan covered in knobbled pills, and rocked back and forth on the bed, watching Tonia with world-weary eyes. "When you on death row, no place for tiptoeing. No place for apologies to the damned."

Her eyes, the color of smoked glass, made her dark skin look ashen. Lula Mae tried to loosen the cornrows braided tight against her scalp, with trembling fingers.

"Bring your chair over," Tonia told her, watching the old woman's achy-looking movements closely. "Got any of that hair cream left?"

She winced as Lula Mae crouched with care, only shaking a little, then tugged a small cardboard box out from under the cot. She extracted a tub of cream and dragged the fragile, plastic folding chair to the door of her cell. The chair had been a gift from the prison, a small acknowledgment the warden and the on-staff physician had made to Lula Mae's advanced age: sitting on the bed for long periods had given her painful back spasms that kept her hunched like a crone for weeks. She eased herself into the padded seat, her back against the bars and to Tonia.

Tonia opened the jar of cream, releasing the fragrance of bergamot and honey to chase away the stale air that trapped frustration, hopelessness, and fear inside. She dipped her fingertips into the cool, dense product and ran the cream over the parched strands.

"Why don't you just tell me what you wanna have? I'm probably gonna be the one to order it anyway." She let her fingers work for a moment. "Unless it's something you want from the cafeteria here."

"I hope you know me better than that."

The indignant tone in the old woman's voice made Tonia laugh. The pure joy in it surprised, then shamed her. How could she find any delight in this moment? "I'd hoped you were getting something good. Something you really want."

"Well, I ain't telling you because I ain't one to steal nobody fun. You like guessing, puzzling things out. I can see that." She tilted her head when Tonia nudged it with the back of her hand to make a straight part in her snow-and-soot hair.

"I do enjoy it, but all I get are nos. I don't even get a hint."

"You ever asked for one?"

Tonia's fingers paused a heartbeat before continuing to braid. "Now that I think about it, I haven't."

Miz Lula Mae grunted. "Hmph. Close mouth don't get fed. Remember that after I'm gone, hear? Always ask for what you want."

Tonia nodded before realizing the woman couldn't see her. "I will," she promised. "But what do *you* want? I need some hint because I haven't guessed in two weeks."

The old woman's head bobbed, and Tonia wondered if she was falling asleep. But she was agreeing. "All right. I'll say this: you thinking too fancy nancy. I'm a simple woman."

"No women are simple," Tonia muttered.

To her surprise, the old woman let out her winter-cough laugh. "Guess you right about that." When she calmed, Lula asked, "So you prefer the company of women?"

Here we go. Miz Lula was from a different time, but that was no excuse for abuse. She prepared herself to correct her sharply, but the woman spoke again.

"Tell you the truth, I do too. Least, I did. Couldn't make up my mind, really." She leaned back into Tonia's hands, which had stilled with shock. "So I kept flitting from pillar to post, not doing nothing much. Then I met Charles Junior, and I thought that was it. Shoulda listened to my ma about one thing: keep pickin and pickin, you gone pick shit."

Tonia smoothed one braid down and parted the hair again from crown to nape. From the smear of cream she'd placed on the back of her hand, she applied a generous dab to the hair. "Did—" She stopped, not wanting to ask the questions she'd been wondering about for the past two years.

"Gone on. I know you got a question in your mouth. Spit it out. Ow!"

Tonia loosened her fingers from pulling too hard on Lula Mae's thinning head of hair. "Sorry," she muttered.

It had been too long since she'd done someone else's hair. It was harder somehow to be gentle when twisting the hair into shape. She was used to using force, tension, to pull her own hair into the place she wanted it, instead of coaxing the strands into line. Her grandmother had been a tenderhead too, flinching when Tonia used too much strength when doing her braids. It was easy to be hard on her own hair, expecting too much from it without replenishing the strands with moisture and oil, ignoring it instead of treating it kindly.

"Were you—are you sorry?"

A stupid question. At least to her own ears. Did it matter whether the woman was sorry now? She wouldn't get the chance to live that decision over again and make a different choice. It was set in stone, and Miz Lula Mae, bearer of pain and indignity and humiliation, would have to bear just a little more for just a little longer. Then . . . well.

"I'm sorry for a lotta things. Sorry I ever met that man. Sorry I let his doings affect me. But I ain't sorry I defended myself."

Tonia dipped her fingers again, spread the slip-slick cream on the section, moved her fingers like the basket weavers back home did. "You sorry he's dead?"

"Yeah," she said. "Cause I'd sure love to haunt his life after I'm gone."

Tonia chuckled. "You wouldn't really haunt him, would you?"

"Oh yes, I would. Make him realize he'd never get rid of me. Not outta his mind, not outta his soul."

Why did everything the doomed said seem so potent? Tonia changed the subject before she could fall into analyzing the words too closely. "You ever had kids?"

"Three. Ain't seen 'em since the trial. Guess they done side with they daddy. Shows what I get for having all girls. They usually sides with they daddy in feuds, you know."

"No, I didn't know. I grew up in a house with all women. Even our dog was female."

"Was you loved?"

"Yes, ma'am."

"That's good, then."

Tonia twisted the end of the final braid and smoothed her palms over her handiwork. "Yeah. But it doesn't mean I had it easy."

"No, or you wouldn't be here now."

"You mean working here?"

"No."

Tonia looked down at her hands. Oiled, they shone like polished blackwood under the yellowed ceiling light. "Didn't think so."

Tonia didn't tell Miz Lula Mae she had been the one sending her those cardboard boxes of toiletries. Seven of them—one a month for each month she'd been covering this wing. She felt sorry for the woman who looked so much like her own grandmother, dead since Tonia was in high school almost a decade before. The similarity was so much it hurt her heart to see the woman roaming the dirty white hallways alone, her hair a neglected tumbleweed. Another prison officer, Judy Daye, told her Miss Lula hadn't ever had a visitor.

"People forget the incarcerated pretty quick," Judy had said to Tonia her first week working the new wing, as she ran her thumbs inside the too-tight waistband of her uniform trousers. "That's how it is. People you used to have some trust in come around for a little while, maybe every week at first. Then it peters off 'til it's nothing. Shame."

After that conversation, Tonia had gone down the road to the Revco drugstore and bought a bottle of cherry-almond body lotion, a jar of Sta-Soft hair cream, a wide-toothed comb, and a box of rubber-tipped bobby pins. On impulse, while she tapped her foot waiting in line, she added a few chocolate bars. She had no idea what Miz Lula liked, so she got a few that had been around a while—Baby Ruths and such.

She wrapped it all up in bubble plastic and tucked it into a brown cardboard box she had left over from a Christmas present too long ago to be remembered. At the last minute, she added a tiny perfume sample she'd gotten in the mail. Some "free gift with purchase" she would never wear. Fragrances weren't allowed on the job, and she never went anywhere else anymore. From the prison to her nice apartment in a not-so-nice neighborhood, where she locked herself in until her next shift.

She'd worked at several places since leaving the army. Local jails, prisons, all in the women's wards as there never seemed to be enough women to watch over other women. Each place she got the same instructions. Don't get too close. Don't get involved. Draw that line in the sand between you and them and don't cross it. Never. And she had listened—up until Miz Lula Mae.

When the women's prison had employed mostly male guards, too much had happened. Too many bloodied pillows, too many gemstone-colored bruises, too many pregnancies. These occurrences plummeted when only women began to handle the female prisoners, in a wave of hiring that included Tonia. They didn't end completely—this was no utopia—but there were fewer. The only thing that stopped was the pregnancies. Although the incarcerated women still got little care, little exercise, little nutrition.

Miz Lula Mae took this upon herself to handle. She scribbled in her scratchy writing a letter to the warden about the quality of food and about her background. She'd worked in school cafeterias most of her youth, only opening her own little place after she'd married.

Didn't need to be expensive food, she'd written. But it needed to be good quality. Not lots of fuss either. Some hearty soups and stews, make the meat go further, do more. Split pea, butter bean, okra, and tomato were all good and cheap and easy to make. Stop throwing away them chicken wing tips and them gizzards. Use them shrimp shells and them beef bones for broth. Good flavor in them bones.

Tonia didn't know if the prison would have done anything with Miz Lula Mae's letter, but somehow a copy of it made its way to the governor's office and some women's rights organization, whose acronym Tonia didn't recognize. An addendum to the letter added that feminine hygiene products were in short supply inside. It took some time, but a new chef soon took over the kitchens. Tonia had seen his close-cropped dark head bent next to Miz Lula Mae's in consultation on several occasions. No one, not even the guards, interrupted these sessions. To be fair, they didn't interrupt her sessions with Miz Lula either. Not now that she'd been scheduled.

The next day, Tonia sat outside the last cell on the left in a folding chair she'd discovered in a closet behind the front guard station. The wearing effects of the extra shifts were taking their toll. It was still early, just after lunch, and the inmates had mostly settled in for their afternoon routines: walks in the yard, TV programs, card games, and shit-talking sessions. They'd had a stomachful, as Miz Lula called it, of rich beef and vegetable chili, fluffy cornbread, and slices of peach pie. After a chorus of thanks for the meal, the normal vibration of activity had descended on the cells.

"Shoulda just opened up my own place by myself and worked at it until I couldn't stand up no more."

"Why didn't you?"

A growl came from the old woman at Tonia's question. "You know, my mama told me I couldn't run no business on my ownsome?"

Tonia's wide-eyed response was enough for the story to continue.

"That's right. Wasn't like y'all got now. You couldn't get no bank account without a man's name on it. You couldn't get a loan or rent a place without a man's name on the papers. And I didn't have no bunch of sisters or women friends wanting to help me."

Miz Lula took a deep breath, and the voice that came from her lips wasn't her own. It was lower, forceful with a no-nonsense edge. It held no tenderness. Tonia imagined the owner of that voice would have made a good prison officer.

"A woman need a man to help with things in a business, Lu. Them white men control everything, and they'll cheat you every chance they get. Now they gonna cheat a Negro man too but not as much as they cheat a woman. They can do more to us. Know what I mean?"

It was hard not to know what Miz Lula's mother had meant.

Tonia leaned her elbows on her knees. "You did the best you could."

The quivering voice was back. "Think so?"

"I know you did."

Lula Mae Heyward lay back on her mattress, her socked feet to Tonia. "I'll put it right one a these days. But now, you ain't had your guesses for the day."

"Duck à l'orange?"

Miz Lula cut her eye.

"Fried chicken?"

"Nope."

"Biscuits and gravy."

"No, ma'am."

Tonia pulled her lower lip between her teeth to keep her words in. But her need was too great and her time too short. *It's not right. It's not polite. When you gonna get another chance?*

"Did you do it?" she blurted.

Lula Mae turned those smoked-glass eyes on her, and Tonia felt a jolt in her chest, right up under her heart. If she'd had her lunch, she would have thought it was indigestion or some hastily devoured mouthful repeating on her. But she hadn't had her break yet. Her stomach had rumbled as she thought of meals Lula might choose, all of them sounding better than the corner store ham-and-Swiss sandwich she'd picked up on the way to work.

"Did I kill him, you askin'?"

Too late to sidestep her question now. *If you bold enough to ask the question, be bold enough to face the answer.* The words of her former sergeant came back to her. Tonia felt like she was looking down a dark, empty barrel at the possibility of an answer she might have to live with for the rest of her life.

What had she expected? That Lula was going to say she hadn't killed her husband and Tonia had twenty-four hours to find his killer? This wasn't a movie of the week. She managed to work her mouth closed and nodded, unsure she wanted to know more.

She didn't have a choice though. Miss Lula had settled in her favorite spot on the bed, far from the wayward spring, into what Tonia had come to know as her storytelling pose. For months, she'd listened to Miss Lula's stories, letting her laughter and indignation show in equal measure at the tales she wove. She squeezed a worm of lotion from the sample tube she kept in her pocket and rubbed it into her hands.

"Well, gone on and get comfortable. Surprised you ain't asked me before."

"I wanted to."

"Why you didn't? Think you being too nosy?"

Tonia nodded again. "Plus, there might be some big, painful story you didn't want to relive."

"It's painful, but it ain't a big story. I left my job to marry a man who started beating my ass on the regular, even before the ink was dry on my marriage certificate. Nobody gave a damn. For years. Decades. Not until I hit him back. Then everybody mouth had something to say. By then, he was dead, and I was in here."

"How long?"

"How long was I married or how long he beat me?" She smoothed a hand over her neat rows of braids. "Same answer, I guess. Twenty-some-odd years."

Tonia saw Ferrar strutting down the hallway past the guard's breakroom while she took the chill off her sandwich in the microwave. Her lunch break had vanished; it was now the dinner hour, and she still hadn't eaten. Her day had been a long haul—answering a call for assistance from another wing when a fight broke out had taken over most of her shift: pulling the women apart, taking a clip on the chin herself, and getting everyone corralled back into their cells had sapped a lot of her energy. Seeing Ferrar's jaunty attitude grated on the last nerve she had left.

"What you so happy about?"

"Might get off that desk yet."

Tonia sucked her teeth. "You mean you did some actual work."

"Work you woulda had to do if you wasn't out there dealing with catfights." A glee-filled grin slipped across his face, and Tonia's stomach roiled.

"I'm tired, Ferrar. Just say what you gotta say."

"Your friend's last meal is tomorrow night."

"I know."

"Then she goes to—"

"Have the injection. I know."

He pointed his finger in her direction, and she wanted to bite it off. "You don't know. See? Talk too much and don't listen."

"Ferrar!"

He sulked but couldn't hide how proud he was of his assignment. "She ain't getting no injection."

Her heart was in a jar of molasses, struggling to beat. "There was a pardon?"

"Don't she wish? Nah." He waved his hand—*gone with that foolishness.* "The box of injection drug they got is outta date, and they can't get no more no time soon."

Already Tonia was moving toward the door to the breakroom, her meal forgotten.

"All y'all guards was on the other side, so they had to find someone to tell her." He noticed the abandoned sandwich, raised his eyebrows. "She gotta choose how to go: the chair or the firing squad."

Tonia was running.

"Hey!" Ferrar shouted after her. "I can eat this?"

Her lungs burned, but Tonia pushed herself forward, feet pounding against the unforgiving stone floor. Chin throbbing, side stitching. When Tonia got to the wing, she could hear the other inmates whispering, their gazes accusing. She only stopped running when she got to the last cell on the left. Dragging in lungfuls of air, she stood with an arm against the bars, panting, trying to bring words to her lips.

"You heard?"

All Tonia could do was nod.

Lula Mae's cackle echoed off the three stone walls of her cell. "First choice I had since I got here. You gotta laugh, don't cha? Just to keep from cryin'."

Tonia lowered her head, shook it. "Wh-what are you going to do?"

"I don't know, chile. Think, I suppose. Sit here and think." Miz Lula leaned back against the wall in her storytelling pose. But there weren't going to be any stories tonight. "Go on home now. Your shift must be over."

"Crabcakes?"

Lula's eyes widened for a moment, then she shook her head.

"Okra soup?"

"No, darlin'. This your last guess now. Make it a good one."

Tears welled in Tonia's eyes, and she had to fight them back. There was a saying that when an elder dies, a library closes. All her stories, her knowledge, her years . . . all of that would be gone within seconds. She'd consoled herself that once the needle went in and the poison hit Miz Lula's bloodstream, it would be over gently. But who knew? The drug held a paralytic, so actual death could be excruciating. And no one would know.

Now, even that soft option was no more. It was the chair or the gun. Miz Lula would not be going quietly into that good night. Eighty years of life, fighting and winning, striving and losing—gone forever. She wished she'd known her longer. She wished she had more time.

Tonia felt the old woman's hand on her arm.

"Don't cry, gal. Some of us come here with nothin' but our good name, and we leave with less. That's all. That's all it is."

Her chest burned. The years she'd spent chasing dreams of wealth and having the life everyone else thought she should have. The stupid idea that she could do what she wanted without it affecting anyone else in the world. It all felt like a waste of energy, a waste of time.

"I don't know what to guess. I"—she cleared her throat—"I'll need your order of food anyway, so you might as well tell me."

"You sure?"

Tonia nodded.

"You gonna kick yourself. I want you to get me a Number 11 barbeque plate from Russell's."

Shock dried the tears in Tonia's throat. "B-barbeque? You want a barbeque plate?"

When the woman nodded, Tonia almost laughed. Would have had she not been so torn apart.

"Why didn't I think of that?"

"Cause you got a fixed idea in your mind that you can't see past. You got an idea of what people are supposed to be like instead of watching and listening and learning for yourself. I'd think they'd break you out of that in whatever training they do for this job."

Funnily enough, there was little information on listening in the training for this job. There was a lot of instruction on how to handle riots, aggressive inmates, fights. How to be watchful for attack. Where the safety exits were. But precious little on listening to the inmates. Once you were here, out of the police station, out of the courtroom, no one needed to listen.

"I guess it wasn't the first thing on my mind."

"Or the twentieth."

"You right."

"And I'ma have my plate soon." She reached through the bars and grabbed Tonia's arm, her grip strong for one so thin. Her eyes burned fever bright. "You gonna get it, right?"

"Of course." She spoke soothingly, as if to a panicked child. Miz Lula's grip eased, and she drew away, head down, until she was once again sitting on her mattress, back to the wall.

"Appreciate you," she muttered to the thin blanket.

After wiping the tears from her cheeks, Tonia stood. Her uniform felt uncomfortable. Sweaty and snug. She put it out of her mind. Tomorrow night, Miz Lula Mae would have what she wanted for dinner, then go into a special, separate private cell overnight—to be executed the next morning.

Warden Manigault was on the phone, but she looked up and waved Tonia inside, indicating she should sit across the desk from her. The warden had a perpetual stone face, her skin the color of fresh-cut applewood before it dried into usable chips. Built tall and broad, she was a presence that filled a room with power, and Tonia felt it keenly. She'd never been called into the warden's office before, not at this job or her previous ones. She kept her head down, did her work, followed procedure. She did not get in trouble.

When Manigault put down the phone, Tonia crossed her ankles tight.

"I hear you've taken a liking to one of the inmates here."

A liking? "Lula Mae Heyward, yes."

Warden nodded. "That is an action discouraged here, Officer. We do not begin relationships with the inmates. Platonic or otherwise."

"Yes, Warden."

"Why?"

Tonia started. "Why?" she repeated.

When the warden didn't acknowledge her question, she rushed to fill the gap of silence. "I . . . she's old, and she has no one. I mean, no one visits her."

"You felt sorry for her. I understand." Warden leaned back in her chair and slid it along the floor to a battered filing cabinet. From a loop on her hip, she pulled a key and fitted it to the lock. "It can't happen again though. Do you understand me?"

"Yes'm."

"Good. I had a grandmother too. Learned a lot from her, but I had her longer than your file says you had yours. Your grandmother raised you?"

Tonia nodded. Her parents had been street runners, loving the night and the brief pleasure it brought before the pain. Her father had been gunned down outside a nightclub, and her mother had left her wrapped in a worn, stained sweatshirt with her own mother and had never returned. It was possible she was still alive, but Tonia had never bothered to check.

"It's a hard thing to care about those we watch over. Total apathy isn't the answer either."

"What is?"

Warden looked up from the manila file folder in her hands. "When I figure it out, I'll tell you. Hell, I'll send out a memo. Here." She lay a sheet of paper on the desk. "Fill this out, so we can have record that you're leaving to pick up the last meal and attend the execution. Disclose any conversations you've had that are pertinent. Press hard—it needs to make four copies."

Tonia completed the form, her fingers aching from exerting pressure. Under "relevant information shared by inmate," Tonia wrote "N/A".

Warden checked the form over, tore off the top sheet, slid the rest into her outbox. "She decided what she wants yet?"

"Barbeque."

"Good choice," Warden said, turning around in her chair to face the window overlooking the courtyard.

Tonia had been dismissed.

Outside for the first time in hours, Tonia inhaled a great gulp of air. It was hot—still so hot even after five, but it was fresher air than she had been breathing since she arrived on shift. She drove through the parking lot and out of the gates, nodding to the guard on duty. Warden had given her the state card to pay for the food, telling her to get a receipt. If she could, she would have paid for the meal herself, but Warden's look stopped the request before she could make it.

The roads were heavy with traffic, people knocking off from work and fighting to get home. Tonia tapped her foot as she navigated the thick rows of cars, shifting and positioning herself to get to the exit as quickly as possible. Maybe she'd have to take another route to get to the restaurant.

She'd had to ask Judy for directions, and the older white woman had looked at her closely before answering. Slowly and carefully, she printed down the directions on a receipt she'd found in her breast pocket.

"Call me if you get lost, okay?"

Bemused, Tonia agreed, but her sense of direction was strong, and she wasn't worried. Besides, if what Miz Lula said was true, she'd smell the fragrance way before she saw the place.

Once she exited the highway, she passed several abandoned buildings, disused gas stations, and empty parking lots. Burned-out cars littered the roadways, and what businesses were still open and functioning took precautions: windows and doors were covered in ironwork bars, and closed-captioned TV cameras covered front doors. Even so, many windows had been broken and repaired with duct tape or covered over with plywood.

Tonia cracked her windows enough to be able to follow her nose when time came. The sun was creeping toward setting, and streetlights flickered, not quite ready or able to come on and bring some illumination to the coming night.

Cold air from the car's air conditioning blew on her face, making the sweat on her brow chilly. Judy's directions lay on the seat next to her, and she glanced at them enough to see there was one more turn. A left on Columbia Street.

When she pulled up a few moments later, it was after following her nose. Nerves had her stomach twisted, but she could recognize and appreciate the scent of smoke and fire and roasting meat dripping into flames.

The building itself was a disappointment. It looked run down enough to be abandoned, if it weren't for the neon "Open" sign with the *e* burned out hanging in the window. And the men—at least four—sitting outside at the rickety-looking picnic table, watching her every move. Their interest had her on edge. Too often, seeing the uniform started mess she didn't want to have to deal with, and now was a time when she had her mental plate full. One of them inserted a toothpick between his one-every-so-often teeth and looked her over carefully as she got out of the cruiser.

"Evenin', Officer," he said around the toothpick. He moved it around in his mouth, took it out, considered it.

"Good evening, gentlemen." The gravel leading up to the door crunched under her feet.

"Come to get somebody?" Mr. Toothpick asked slyly. The others he was with—all of them wiry and taut, sleek-limbed men that may have been anywhere between twenty to forty—chuckled with him. Their faces were obscured: some by battered baseball caps pulled low, others by the setting sunlight, framing them from behind.

"Just here for a plate," Tonia said. Was this gonna turn into a situation? "Come to grab my Number 11."

The men looked startled, and Mr. Toothpick's grin faded. His friends looked at her and pulled their hats off, mumbling some words under their breath Tonia didn't catch. Before she knew it, Toothpick had stood and was marching toward her. He reached out, and she felt her body tense, readying itself. But he only opened the door for her.

"Have a good night, Officer. Get back safe."

She looked at his hand on the door handle, back at his now serious face.

"Thank you."

Outside Russell's was a prophecy to the inside of the place. Run-down, surely—the air conditioning units protested loudly—but scrubbed clean. Despite the chips in their surface, the Formica countertops glowed, and underneath the mouth-watering scent of food, there lay a faint ghost of pine cleaner. Tonia counted five tables inside, all four-seaters. Of the remaining chairs, only a lucky few existed without damage of some kind. Most had help holding in their stuffing with colored duct tape.

Jovial voices from the back room behind the counter mixed with the metallic clank of tongs and spoons against bowls. The occasional burst of cackling laughter. Every few moments, a different woman would emerge from that back room with a brown paper bag or a foil-covered tray and send off an eager customer with a sweet, quick smile and what sounded like real thanks. Three people stood in line before her, allowing Tonia to scan the large white peg board with black letters, listing the food available:

BBQ Combo	Chicken QTR HALF WHOLE
BBQ Plate #1, #2, #7, #9	Rack HALF WHOLE
BBQ Dinner	Slaw, Salad, Beans
	Half-Pint Pint

So it was that kinda place. No description of anything. No prices. Either you asked what each menu item contained, or you just chose and got what was given. Didn't matter. She wasn't here for herself, and she knew her order already. Her stomach rumbled though. Should she get something for herself as well? Next time maybe. She wasn't going to mess with this all-too-important order, especially when using the warden's card.

The last few days had played with her mind so much, she couldn't sleep through the nights or finish her store-bought meals—worried about Miz Lula and what her own life would be like at the prison without her there.

Had she chosen yet? It was a hellafied choice: the chair or the gun. In the same position, Tonia didn't know which she would pick. Neither one had the edge over the other in her mind.

"Next!"

The sharp command jolted Tonia out of her imaginings. Belatedly, she realized there was no #11 listed on the board. She hustled up to the counter where a tall, brown-skinned, sour-faced young woman stood behind the register, impatient. Weight on one hip, the woman looked Tonia up and down, clearly finding her unimpressive. She parted her lips and cracked her gum on her back teeth, the sound splitting the air like gunshot.

"What you want?"

Tonia took the high road in responding. No need to follow up this woman. She was here on a singular mission: to bring Miz Lula her requested food and make her last meal the most comforting she could. Who knew how the woman might mess with the food if this turned into . . . something.

"I don't see the thing I was asked to order."

The woman's lips tightened, and she draped her wrist on top of the register, her brass bracelets releasing a wind chime of sound into the overheated room. "So get something else."

This heifer . . .

Tonia kept her face neutral. She wanted to smile but couldn't manage it, not at the moment. Lord, why couldn't even this be easy? "I can't. I'm here for a Number 11, and I need to get it—or something as close to it as possible."

Tonia and her new nemesis stared at each other for a good ten seconds before the woman broke their stand off and asked, "Who for?"

"What?"

A labored sigh paired with an eye roll this time. Who thought it was a good idea to have this person on the register? "Who the food for?"

There was no reason not to say. The papers and the news had been carrying the story for weeks. *First State Execution in Twenty Years. Justice Finally Served in Brutal Beating Death. Black Domestic Violence Survivor to Face the Needle.* While no one visited her during her incarceration, Miz Lula was for the moment a household name.

"Lula Mae Heyward."

The woman, whose sour face had morphed into stone, blew a big pink bubble while she stared at Tonia. She sucked it back in with force, the bubble collapsing in on itself with an impressive snap. Then she left the register and walked into the back room, leaving Tonia to wonder with the hell was going on. The clanging of metal on metal stopped for a moment, as did the chatter. Strange, the sudden silence. Then the sounds of the BBQ joint were back and so was ol' sour face.

She quoted Tonia a price, took the card, and handed over a receipt. Then she switched herself over to the panel that separated her from the clientele and pulled it open.

"Go on back."

Jaw slowly working on the gum, the woman gestured to the door of the room she'd disappeared through a moment ago. Unsure of what she was about to encounter, Tonia steeled herself with the reminder that this was not for her. It was for Miz Lula. She forced her steps forward.

Ol' Sour Face called, "Next!" and the sound of business out front resumed.

Behind Tonia, the panel shut and locked. Her work shoes made no sound on the linoleum, even where it was lifting in spots and caught the edge of the door as it swung. On the other side of the door, three women of various shades greeted her with tender eyes and soft words. The youngest stood at a stove over an enormous stockpot, the steam rising off the contents making her edges curl. The oldest sat at a metal table: a knife, small and sharp, in one hand. A coil of potato peel lolled off the blade to the tabletop. The final one was in the mouth of an open pantry, hand on a clear canister of dark-red powder. It was this last woman who gestured toward a battered but solid-looking door that must lead outside.

"Pitmaster's that way."

When Tonia placed her hand on the doorknob, it was hot to the touch. Hot enough that for a moment she feared what was beyond it. She glanced back to the three women, confused and unsure.

"Gone on, now. Your choice ain't near as hard as hers."

Ain't that the truth.

Tonia turned the doorknob and stepped outside onto bare black soil. The door thudded closed after her, making her jump. She faced the fire.

The literal fire.

A circle of black oil drums, halved, sat on metal stands. The heat was immense, too swollen to be contained in these outdoors, and it filled Tonia up until she was gasping. Clean smoke blossomed from every container, every grill top, obscuring Tonia's vision. Her stomach protested loudly at being denied.

"Here for pickup?"

The Pitmaster's contralto voice carried over the roar of the flames and the hiss of fat touching fire. Since the sun hadn't quite set, there was still watercolor light in the sky, and there would be for another few hours. Despite that, the smoke and leaping flames forced Tonia to squint to see the woman behind the voice as she replied.

"Yes, ma'am."

She should be able to see the Pitmaster better than she was. No matter where Tonia moved to try and improve her vantage point, her view of the woman remained shrouded. Tall and broad of shoulder and hip, the woman moved smoothly, steadily between the grills and the pit dug into the earth behind her. She glided as if she weren't bound by gravity, Tonia thought, but surely, it was only the coiling smoke off the pit, the pinkening sun behind streaks of cloud, turning the sky into raw hog jowl, and the lengthening shadows of canopy of live oak trees tricking her eyes. Sweet, dark smoke filled her and her mouth watered.

Tongs snapped, gripped, metal jaws reflecting the flames. Tonia jerked, having been lost in the scene before her. Maybe not even there. Maybe she'd been lost in some other place, some other time where she wasn't herself for a cause. Somewhere where Miz Lula wasn't making an impossible decision. Maybe she was lost in another world where the only decisions were what to smell, what to sip, what should lay on the tongue. What number to choose.

Numbers were why she was here in the first place. Miz Lula's number was up, wasn't it? And there wasn't anything Tonia could do except make this last gift to her. Pick up a tray of food and deliver it. What kinda mission was that? What kinda thing to do as a final act? It was nothing. Really.

"No, not nothing."

Tonia turned to the contralto voice, stentorian above the flames. "Excuse me?"

"It ain't nothing. This final act you doing. Girl. More'n anyone else has."

There was nothing Tonia could say to that. "If you know her so well, why didn't you ever visit her? She's been there twenty years." The rage in her voice mirrored the roar of the flames.

A clink and a searing hiss met her words. "I visit how I can, in dreams and in visions, in the faraway expressions that take her away from this side for a few moments. When that happens, I am there with her. But I cannot leave here. I stay with the fires. They emerge here, and I use them, so they do not consume too much too fast."

Another clink of metal on metal and the hiss of fire kissing flesh. When the Pitmaster moved, Tonia could see . . . something propelling her. Not legs exactly . . . then it was shrouded again in smoky mists. Her head spun. Smoke coiled around her; she knew her hair, her skin, her lungs were absorbing it, but she couldn't avoid its reach. A craving unlike any she'd ever felt blossomed inside her, and she had to swallow down the saliva forming in the deepest corners of her mouth.

"This food, this meat and wegetable and fruit, it slows down the fire." The Pitmaster's voice reached her from what felt like a great distance. "No more water, the fire next time. Remember that? Well, the fire is already here. Been here. It consumes no matter what. Sometime it takes too quick, on those days where evil just seem to win, searing those in its path. Those that die by fire die . . . in such agony. There are those like me who tend the fires where they emerge. Back them off for a little while."

A glut of flame split the earth, rising from the ground in a plume of destruction. Tonia yelled, threw herself back from the geyser. But the Pitmaster took up the searing-hot grill in her hands and moved it over the split in the earth. A slab of meat from a cooler went on, and Tonia could have sworn she heard a sigh.

"No, I cannot go anywhere, girl. My duty is here. And yours is out there."

The Pitmaster took a metal tray, filled it with several select pieces while Tonia watched, dumbfounded. "Is this the only place standing between us and the end?"

"Not the only but one of the few. Enjoy your life, girl. Take this to her."

Without thinking, without intending to, Tonia held out her hands to receive the package. It was heavy for its size. "What is it?"

It was impossible to tell if the sigh came from the pit or its master. "What she wants."

The metal tray was hot but not unbearable on her bare hands. She backed away from the Pitmaster who was now engrossed again at tending her eternal fires. Briefly she wondered where the other fires were and who was tending them in order to give the world one more chance to prove itself. Did it matter though? Someone was holding the line, making food to sustain us from the very thing meant to kill us all. Making a way where there was no way to be made.

"I'm grateful to you."

Tonia swallowed hard, not expecting a response, and raced back inside the door to Russell's. It closed behind her, and she leaned her back against it, sweat running down under her bra strap and into the elastic waistband of her briefs. Her breathing came fast now, fast as if she had run miles, and she had only spoken with the woman—creature, goddess—who had tended the flames and chose Lula Mae's last meal. What would this food do to her?

What she wants it to.

The three women were staring at her when Tonia came back to herself. One of them, the one who had directed her outside, approached and placed the metal tray in a bag, along with paper containers of fixins Tonia didn't have the heart or mind to inquire about. The woman placed the full brown paper bag in Tonia's outstretched arms like it was a baby.

"Number 11," she said, nudging Tonia toward the door.

On stiff, wooden legs, Tonia left the kitchen, trailed by the scent of smoke. Through the door that separated the kitchen from behind the counter, where she stared at Ol' Sour Face, who lifted the barrier, allowing her to leave. To return to the old/young men outside and to Toothpick, who opened the door to release her from the strangeness of Russell's and out into the fresh bathwater-hot air. She breathed a smoke-filled thanks and let herself into the car where cold air conditioning hit her in the face like a slap bringing her out of a trance. She sat the brown paper bag on the seat next to her and buckled it in. After a long look at the door of Russell's, Tonia started the engine and returned to the prison.

She drove with the sound of evening approaching as her soundtrack, the window open even with the AC on. The smell of the food was so intoxicating, her stomach clenched hard enough to make her gasp. Her jaw worked of its own accord as if she had just torn off a piece of meat from the bone and was moaning at the salty savor that washed over her tongue.

Need gripped her, the urge to pull over to the side of the road and wedge the container open and pinch off a scrap. A taste of that seared, smoky, delicacy after a steady diet of store-bought, plastic-wrapped sandwiches would be a bliss. Her hands gripped ten and two, and her foot pressed the accelerator. The brown paper bag rippled in the wind as she drove, and a feeling washed over her like she was fleeing from something too large to understand.

Lula Mae ate alone while Tonia and another guard waited outside the room. She hadn't gotten a drink, so Tonia supplied a cold RC Cola from the vending machine. Miz Lula ate slowly but consistently for the better part of an hour. Even with the white plastic spoon and fork and her trembling hands, she made a decent job of it.

Tonia gathered the empty, still-warm metal trays while the other guard kept watch over Miz Lula. There was no need for concern: the old woman only rocked back and forth in her chair, a small smile of contentment on her face.

"Musta been good," the guard remarked.

Miz Lula kissed her fingertips. "Beef brisket marinated and rubbed and smoked slow until the cap of fat melts, basting that meat 'til you can look at it sideways and it falls apart. Fall off the bone ribs so good your heart break when you look and see the plate empty."

"Now that makes me wish I gotten some for myself."

Miz Lula turned her gaze to Tonia. It was a long stare, over and through and far away. "Always hold something back for yourself. Some little part, some tiny speck that you can cradle and know is all yours. Something just for you."

"Miss Lula," Tonia started toward her.

"Gone now," she said, waving a hand to shoo both guards away. "Lemme digest my food."

The guards left the prisoner to sit on the mattress without rips or loose springs. Tonia would be there in the morning for . . . whatever Miz Lula decided.

"Did you hear if she chose her . . ." Tonia couldn't bring herself to finish the question, instead waving a hand in a limp gesture before returning it to her belt. The strength of it usually felt grounding, secure, but now it weighed on her, tugging at her belly.

The other guard scratched at her scalp with both hands. "Nah, I didn't hear nothing. It's a shame before the Lord though. If she won't choose, they'll do it for her in the morning."

"What do you think they'll pick?"

"Oh, the chair."

She rubbed her lips together. "Really? Why?"

"The way they keep that thing serviced and polished and in perfect condition? Sure, they'll use it. Come on now. That chair got its own inside circle of operators who know how to maintain it. Like some kinda exclusive club." The guard shuddered and gave Tonia a sidelong glance. "You gonna attend?"

She said it like the execution was invitation only, a wedding or some state dinner. Tonia thanked God she had company; she ached to run her finger in the juices left in the warm metal trays and suck it clean. She swallowed. "Yeah, I'll be there."

The next morning the prison was in an uproar. When they went to get Miz Lula Mae, she was already gone. Not disappeared but gone to glory. They'd tested the contents of her stomach: no drugs, no poison, she had died of natural causes. Her body in repose was peaceful. Her arms tucked close to her body as if she was clutching something no longer there.

The guards were watching and re-watching the footage from the cameras overlooking the cell. Nothing out of the ordinary, nothing to cause concern. It was an eighty-year-old woman, what could they do? It was the stress of the situation, they decided. How would they spin this? What would they tell the press who were already gathered for the execution—for their portion of her?

Tonia stood frozen in the corner of the death room where the chair waited. It was what they'd decided for her. It was clearly the best solution in their estimation, and now what? While there were a few faces showing relief, anger swept throughout the majority of those gathered. They'd been denied. Denied the right to . . . what?

Feeling eyes on her, Tonia glanced over to see Warden Manigault regarding her. They locked gazes for a moment, and Tonia wondered if the warden thought she'd had something to do with this. Tonia herself wondered as well. What had happened? There was no reason to think the food had been magically spiked with some seasoning, some spices that would allow a person to expire when they were ready. It would have been found in the chem test of her stomach contents. There was going to be an autopsy, of course. Miz Lula's body would be held for investigation, dissected, pulled apart to see . . . well, just to see. No one would be coming to claim for the body, so it didn't matter.

Finally, Warden Manigault broke the stare and turned her attention to the multitude of guards, officials, and press clamoring for answers. And Tonia was able to skulk away and do her job. The last cell on the left was empty now, swept, hosed, scrubbed. The other inmates whispered among themselves, casting suspicious glances toward Tonia. They could wonder all they wanted. She'd done nothing.

By the end of her shift, Tonia was bone tired. Her mind a mush, her muscles tighter and stiffer than wire. She headed home, soaked in the bath, then ate a pint of vanilla ice cream, drowned in what was left of a fifth of brandy. Miz Lula was gone. Her grandmother was gone. She was still here. Why? A small hunger chewed away in the back of her mind. She slept and dreamed of fire-warmed metal enclosing her like a casket. Melting her flesh into something new. In the dream, she awoke from it renewed, a covenant between her and the flames. *Next time*, it said. *Next time.*

Tonia expected to get called into Warden Manigault's office the next day, and she had a triple shot of espresso to prepare herself. Only the talk didn't come at the beginning of the day when she was prepared for it. It came at the end of her shift when she was already worn, grief creeping into her bones, hunger knotting her stomach.

"You said the inmate had nothing specific to say the day before execution." The Warden's gray eyes in her browned butter face were stern, assessing.

"Correct."

"Nothing at all."

"She said stuff but nothing unusual. Nothing important."

"How do you gauge important?"

"I interpreted that to mean about her case or something illegal. Not if she wanted sauce on the side or not." Weariness made her tongue sharp, and she held her breath after her tart reply to her boss's question.

Warden's lips thinned, and she tapped her pen on the desk. "This is irregular, Officer. Highly irregular."

After twenty years without an extension, what was regular? Tonia had done nothing. They had no proof she did, and she sure as hell wasn't going to say she had. Warden Manigault made her go through the experience of leaving the prison, picking up the food, and returning five times. Detail by detail, turn by turn. Each time, Tonia recited it all, except for the Pitmaster. An eternity passed before Warden turned off the tape recorder.

"You can go, Officer."

"I'm . . . still . . ."

"Employed, yes. This wasn't a hearing. You weren't being charged. We just needed to cover all of the bases. I'm sure you understand."

Then why did it feel like a trial? "Of course, Warden."

Tonia floated through the last few minutes of her day, wondering now what the prison would be like. Ferrar had put in for a transfer to the men's ward, and it looked like he would be getting it. She was glad, not just to be rid of him but for someone achieving their dream. What was hers? Did she even know anymore? She would settle for—

No, no need to finish that sentence.

She would do what she wanted. Now to figure that out. Tonia left work with no idea of where she was going or what she was doing. She just drove.

The sky was still draped in indigo when Tonia pulled up in front of Russell's. There was no line now, and the place seemed empty. She circled the building in her car twice, not seeing what she'd beheld earlier. No flames emerging from the ground. No Pitmaster. None of it. Still, the scent of barbeque lingered in the air, a reminder.

She parked and walked up to the building. How had she seen what she'd seen? It didn't make sense. She eased herself into a seat at one of the wooden picnic tables. Stared at the door, wondering if she had for a few moments given into grief and let some fantasy of a way to allow Miz Lula a second chance play out in her mind.

Starlight draped the sky, and a cool breeze moved around the scattering of cloud cover. Tonia loosened the top two buttons on her uniform shirt to get the benefit of the night air on her overheated skin. A match flared to life in the darkness across from her, and she turned toward it with a barely suppressed gasp.

"Look like you looking for something."

The match touched a cigarette, and a halo of light illuminated Ol' Sour Face. She then lit a small candle on the table where she sat, and it gave off a red glow as she shook out the match.

"No, not really. I'm . . . just hoping it will find me."

The woman chuckled, and Tonia realized she liked the sound, a husky warmth that belied her earlier impression. "Maybe it will."

"You sure have changed your tune."

"Ain't no line of people hollerin' orders at me. I gotta keep people in check."

"Don't I know it," Tonia said, laying her heavy head in her palm. That was the entire purpose of her job, keeping people in check. Because steel bars weren't enough to do so. Neither was the threat of hundred-year-old chairs or tubes of expired liquid death. She didn't want to keep anyone in check anymore. Especially not herself.

"You closed?"

The woman lifted a thinly arched brow. "Why? You hungry?"

Tonia stared at the woman for an eternity, a slow pulse thumping to life in a place she'd thought dead and decayed. Insensate. She rubbed her lips together.

Keep something back for yourself.

Wherever she was, Tonia hoped Miz Lula was doing just that. Living well in this her next life. But keeping some small part of herself to herself. Just for her.

She nodded. "For a long while now."

A long drag on the cigarette, a tap of ashes on the concrete before Tonia's companion stood, swung her legs from under the picnic table, and unlocked the door, holding it open for Tonia. "Then let's get you fed."

One if by Sea

YOU WANT YOUR LITTLE GIRL BACK OR NOT?

I'ma tell you how to do it. Get your life back the way it was. No more of that cold, empty hole lyin' in your belly.

Why you cryin'? I done told you I was gonna help fix it. Just keep my name outta your mouth and it all gonna be fine.

You wanna go by land or sea? Don't ask 'bout air. Air is too hard and I'm old—ain't got the strength to help more than I already am.

Sea? Good, then.

Dress in white. To let the dead know your intentions is pure. And it might save you a bit of time, make the spirits think you one of 'em for a while. Or it might make 'em angry and wanna bind you there. I don't know what's in the minds of the dead.

Bathe in blue water. Soak in it from your hair to your toes. Hell, paint your toenails blue. While you in that water, pray to your god-lady: Oshun, Mami Wata, whoever it is you follow. Ask for guidance.

Listen for her words, then lay yourself back in that tub there. Cling to them words because once you pass through the water, you gonna be outta my reach. When you get pulled down through the tub, don't fight. If you done it right, you won't drown. If you done it wrong, well . . . I'll light candles for your soul.

Never said it would be easy. You like too much easy. Sometimes things is just hard. Hush. Hush that cryin' now. I swear all y'all young people who don't know your heart got me vex.

No, that child ain't your heart. Don't ever put that on a child. They grow up and grow apart and live whatever kinda life they want, leavin' you alone. Love 'em, give 'em all you got, then let 'em live. Shoot, you was wantin' to jump in that casket with her.

Where is your heart? They gonna ask that at the big gate. And if you say it's that girl, they'll swing it wide. Then close it behind you 'cause you got what you want, right there in the middle of the beyond. And there you gonna stay in the midst of the dead while they sip at your life until they end you.

No, your daughter ain't your heart. Find somethin' else.

You'll look 'bout close to dead—wet, bedraggled, lost. Should be enough to get you in. Look for her. I don't know where she gonna be, but search everywhere, quiet as you can.

Take this doll. When you find the child, cut some of her hair and plait it into the doll's head. Leave it where you found the girl.

Pick her up, drag her, so long as you got your arms around her. I know she's heavy. Gonna be heavier with the death weight on her. No, don't hold her hand. Fingers is too easy to break.

Don't see no reason to put sugar on it. You gonna have to fight to get out. The moment them dead know you tryin' to take one a theirs, they'll be after you. Run, fast as you can, 'til your lungs 'bout to burst. Push 'em away. Kick. Protect your chest, protect that girl, and remember your heart—what you got to come back to.

Go on, I ain't got all night.

I'll be waitin'. . . for whatever come up through that blue water.

Witches for Mars

N O ONE EXPECTED THE GOVERNMENT TO ALLOW IT. TO ACKNOWLEDGE it even, but Maira looked at the advertisement above a webpage she used to compare prices of agate and selenite healing crystals.

Witches for Mars. Must be practicing full, knowledge-grounded, not learning.

"Practicing full?" Maira scoffed into her cup of catnip tea laced with a few spoonfuls of blue aster honey, the only breakfast she allowed herself from her dwindling supply of food. If a witch was worth anything, learning never stopped. We were the wild ones—the ones who listened to the stories ancient trees whispered, who hummed the tunes Auntie Wind made when she whistled through the fields.

Another sip of tea. People feared what they didn't understand. Many merchants refused to sell food to witches, claiming the magic-touched had poisoned the Earth in the first place, withering crops, sickening animals, tainting water reserves. Maira laughed without humor. The more things changed and all that. It was difficult to accept your participation in your own demise.

Maira had taken to growing her own benne crop, which was more resistant to drought, and the flat biscuits she made with the ground seeds and oil were her main source of protein and fat. But she missed the days of having slices of airy bread, toasted to a hot crunch, slathered with sweet-cream butter to accompany her tea.

For a moment, she was lost to this world as she stared out of her opened sheer-paneled curtains into the eye-watering brightness of midday. Poppet Street was empty, but why wouldn't it be? There were no more witch covens in Charleston. No more neighborhoods where spells were bartered and borrowed, where children learned Earth and ancestor reverence along with maths and sciences. No more block parties under full moonlight, no more sweetcakes, no more front porch conventions, where elders in ankle-length capes strode across the broom-swept street, barefooted, to mediate disputes.

Plywood now covered the windows of most houses, their salt-blasted boards flaking paint onto broken steps and overgrown azalea bushes. The air was sweet with floral-laced decay. Only her small carriage house and Algin's next door were still occupied.

It was a place she didn't recognize and one she rarely ventured into anymore. While the world had never been truly accepting of witchkind, there used to be pockets of tolerance where it was possible to live, even thrive. Now assaults rose to fill the gap, and it turned Maira's stomach.

When she'd been a witchling, no more than six or seven, the elders told stories of how those without magic had killed her ancestors—burnings, hangings, drownings, and so, so many other ways. Maira was glad she lived in different times, when people were more accepting, and on one occasion said as much.

Her great-grandpap's summoned spirit had answered through her mother's lips. "Don' be sho, gal. Dey mines can change in a flick of a hosstail 'bout we. Den you guh see."

She'd lowered her gaze from the whites of her mother's eyes while she held Papa Daddy's spirit and channeled his words. She couldn't fight the battles her ancestors had. She wasn't strong. She wasn't able to face the scorn and hatred.

Wherever Papa Daddy was, he was probably looking at her saying, "Well, yuh facin' it nah, ain'tcha?"

Certainly she wasn't as bad off as some. The news showed witch-owned houses and shops vandalized, her people beaten and violated. What had started in small cells, patches in rural towns and villages, finally spread to major cities. Her belly churned and she sipped more tea to ease it.

Maira pulled a shawl around her shoulders. The more the flames of anger and hate spread, the colder she got. Why us? We were the ones who spoke of Earth's end and bore the weight of the world's jeering. That scathing ridicule had turned to fear-soaked wails and frantic scrabbling for what used to be. Too late . . . too late, baby. Buh-bye.

Maira slammed the teacup back down into its saucer, then winced before she checked for damage. None. She turned her inspection back to the computer screen. This advertisement on a website that had few visitors—it sold specifically to licensed witcheren—was odd. Was it real? She hovered her cursor over the banner to see the URL it linked to. Gibberish. Probably a virus meant to destroy her computer. She wouldn't put it past some of the people out there, so entrenched in their desire to eliminate the magical.

She went into the kitchen, the warmest place in her house. The kitchen had been Muffin's favorite room, a snug place of treats and sun-filled windows. Once the witch persecutions began, so did the cat destructions. They hadn't lasted long. One day, all the felines disappeared: from homes, from shelters, from zoos. They were the wild ones, too. And they had fled. She missed her Muffin, but she understood. Save yourself. It was all about that in the end.

Maira held her hands over the largest eye of the stove, rubbed her palms together. The heat cheered her a little, and the heavy fog inside her lifted. She didn't have to decide anything in this moment or even at all today. Today, she would go out and take advantage of the clear sky and nature's gifts before the pickings got slim. Her stomach rumbled, and that was decided. They were few, but they were not alone and those that waited to search the surrounding woods often did without.

She and Algin used to forage together, the sun beating down on their bare heads, warming their hair oils until the fragrance of roasting sesame surrounded them, but since that kid had thrown acid in her face, Algin hadn't left Poppet. Maira went alone these days. She shoved her feet into shoes, grabbed her paw print messenger bag. She gulped the rest of her tea, then headed out.

Maira hitched the brown paper bag further up on her hip. It would break soon, but it would hold long enough for her to get home. Three streets up, one street over. Twenty minutes, tops.

Today had been a good day. Blackberries abounded, their skins taut and shiny. The wild strawbs she found were ripe but didn't smoosh in her fingers when she plucked them from their viney beds. Honeysuckle blossoms, their teardrop of sweetness enough to forgo some of the precious sugar. Dandelion greens, plump figs, an assortment of papershell pecans, accompanied rosehips and saw palmetto leaves for tea.

Algin used to love this—the muggy breeze, the sun-hot fruit, the triumph of living off the land. Maira had asked for her company, hoping the peaceful woods would be a balm. She'd even promised to leave during the hottest part of the afternoon when non-witches huddled inside to protect themselves from the harsh sun or skulked in thick cloaks and hoods when they dared venture out. No go. Since the attack, Algin wanted nothing to do with the wider world. So now Maira sat alone on the carpet of grass, leaning her back against a tree trunk as it whispered questions to her.

Why are you here, child?

I was born here. Her thoughts sank into the bark. *My history's here.*

History is not future.

Maira wasn't sure how to respond, and the tree said no more. She sighed, shoved her fingers through her hair. Usually the trees were more willing to share their wisdom. Why would this one suddenly—

She caught a raw, rank scent on the breeze, a sharp stench that made her gorge rise—Auntie Wind telling her what the tree had not. Trouble. Get home. She'd taken too long this time, but the pickings had been fuller than usual, the bloom of summer on the woods.

She stuffed one bulging brown paper bag into her messenger bag and carried the other. Rushing, not running, out of the safe seclusion of the woods, scurrying for the womb-like safety of the clutch. She'd meant to go to the market for milk, hoping for a sympathetic cashier, but a gang of tough-looking men hung around the door, so she skirted the area and chose a route that wound further into the woods before emerging onto pavement.

Maira looked left and right, then jogged across the street, breathing hard. Not from exertion, but from the foul scent the air still carried. She cursed under her breath. Stupid. She should have encouraged Algin more instead of going off alone. Wasn't going it alone that had destroyed the witcheren in the first place?

A flash of color caught her attention, and she stopped. On a telephone pole was another advertisement: this one bearing white lettering printed on red paper.

Witches for Mars!

Below the ornate script was a row of strips, boasting a web address in bold type. No strips had been torn off. Her heart skipped a beat. Maira tore off a strip and stuffed it in her pocket.

She turned away and came face to face with a stranger—more like face to hood as she couldn't see inside the darkened cavern over the person's face. Head coverings weren't unusual, but the inky void within this one felt wrong. The hood turned toward the flyer with its missing strip. The stench blossomed into hate.

It was over fast—the silvery glint of a knife, her yip of pain, her bag dropping to the ground, then footsteps running off into the setting sunlight. Maira grabbed her arm, blood welling between her fingers. She rolled up her sleeve in increments to her elbow, gulping down the spit forming in her mouth. The gash was angry, throbbing, deep. Her skin had separated cleanly—the knife must have been hellishly sharp.

Fuck.

She wiped her hand on her jeans. Used her teeth to wrap a handkerchief around the wound. The white cotton reddened instantly. She picked up her dropped bag and headed for the hospital.

The gash on her arm pulsed as though alive, pulling healing blood from the rest of her body, aided by the agate stone in her front pocket.

A tight-mouthed doctor stitched her up. "How'd you get this?"

"I got attacked." Maira's voice was clipped. The deadness in her arm was unsettling. There was no pain, just the pressure of the needle as it pierced her skin and the *tug tug* of each completed stitch through her insensate arm. She felt disconnected from herself, dulled to all feeling; an observer watching a distant and alien procedure. It incensed her.

The doctor sucked her teeth and muttered something under her breath. The student doc with her gaped, and his weary-looking gaze flicked over to Maira.

"What was that?" she asked. "I didn't hear you clearly."

If Maira had believed the doctor would back off at her sharp words, she was mistaken. The doctor kept her eyes on her work as she spoke. "I said you

shouldn't have been in that part of town anyway. Not like they sell roots or
sticks there."

Maira tried to pull her arm away, but the doctor held it fast. "Be still or you'll
end up worse off than when you came here."

"Let me go." Maira ground the words out from between clenched teeth. Her
veneer of civility dropped to show the face she could only manage when there
was nothing left to care about. She continued, her voice serpent smooth, "Or
you'll be the one worse off."

The woman's eyes went wide, and she lifted her hands into a hold up posture.
She opened her mouth, but Maira snarled, and the doctor's jaw slammed shut
before she stood and walked away without looking back.

Maira watched her leave, then glanced down at the string and needle
swinging from her half-sewn arm. She released her hand from the vial of potion
in her pocket, rubbing the cork to make sure it was still secure. The formula
was Head A Mess—to cause confusion. She was glad she hadn't had to use it on
the not-so-good doctor.

"Um, excuse me."

The verbal nudge came from the student doc. "Yeah?" The feeling still hadn't
returned to her arm, and Maira poked at the half-sutured wound.

"I can finish that," he said. His cheeks were flushed; a bead of sweat on his
brow threatened to slide behind the frame of his glasses. "I'm qualified."

She shrugged and replaced her arm on the table. He nodded, almost to
himself, and sat across from her. Maira had words ready to tell him she wasn't
interested in conversation, but he didn't initiate any, instead making even, neat
stitches any tailor would be proud of. Gently, he held her skin together, piercing
the flesh, pulling it until the severed edges kissed.

When finished, he covered the area with a bandage. "All done," he said.

"Thanks." Maira rolled down her ripped sleeve. Looked like she'd be doing
her own sewing tonight. She headed for the door.

"Will you go to Mars?"

She froze, anchored to the floor. "What?"

"It's just that . . . well, my mother is going and I'd worry less if you were there."

"You don't even know me."

"I think I do." He sat on the seat where he'd sewn her together, hands covered
in blue nitrile gloves. "I'm not a witch, but sometimes . . . I see."

Maira grunted, hoisting her bag onto her uninjured arm. "Then you're a witch, Doc. Own it."

Night had fallen. The city was different at full dark. She could hear the wind in the branches overhead, the rustle of leaves when cars zipped by. Her soft-soled shoes made no sound as she walked home, letting the moon ease away the tension of earlier. Not all of it—she had to remain alert in case anyone else lurked, waiting to strike out. It was exhausting, living this way. She wanted to enjoy living.

She winced and switched the bag of food to her other hand. But that wasn't reality, was it? Reality was: be prepared to explain yourself or defend yourself. Most of the time, both.

She made it to her street, and found Algin sitting on her porch steps. Wooly dagger moths darted in and around the watery-yellow lightbulb above the front door, descending to circle around her head like a halo. Where the shadows fell on her face, the skin looked like a landscape, cavernous and pitted in areas, flowing and slick in others.

"Yuh had get los'?" Algin's lulling mix of Gullah and English was a balm after the clipped disapproval in the doctor's tone.

"No, I got stabbed." She showed Algin her bandaged arm, basked in the look of horror that came over her friend's face. A shower of curses followed before Maira could get her to calm down.

"I'm fine, okay?"

"Yuh get jick in da arm, and yuh okay." Algin sucked her teeth, then stretched out a hand. Maira plopped her house key in it. The door tended to stick and she wouldn't be able to open it without hurting herself.

"Drink?" Maira asked once inside, one of the things she could easily do one-handed.

"Please fuh one."

She poured two measures of rectified spirit over ice cubes and topped it with lemon simple syrup and a sprig of thyme from her windowsill. She handed one glass to Algin, and they made themselves comfortable on the covered back porch, sipping.

"I didn't see who did it. They were wearing a hood, then ran off after they cut me."

Algin nodded, pulling up her own hood. She hadn't seen her attacker's face either.

It took Maira almost a week to remember the web address. She'd been keeping loneliness at bay with busy hands and quick feet, bustling around creating, mixing, learning. But today, she was a wild woman alone, craving something. A connection, perhaps.

She dug around and found the clothes she'd been wearing when she took the slip of red paper, and settled herself in front of the computer. The laptop hummed a comforting sound, emitting a mild warmth that added to the coziness of the house. She entered the website and a night sky appeared.

Not on the laptop, that wouldn't have been impressive. A shadow formed outside and overhead, and the bright noontime sky melted to an inky, star-filled indigo.

A voice, tinny and sprightly as an infomercial voiceover, boomed outside: *Witches for Mars! Witches for Mars!*

Startled cries went up in the distance, but Maira didn't listen. She closed her eyes, emptying herself of fear, opening up to the newly formed night. It sparked and sparkled, dark and brilliant.

Then it was gone. She looked at the window, sunlight filling it once again. A skitter of awareness danced along the back of her neck. Someone was talking about her. Or maybe wanted to speak to her.

The doorbell shrieked, and she ran downstairs to peer through the peephole.

"Maira?"

Algin. She opened the door, ushered her friend inside. "You saw what happened?"

"Yep."

"And?"

Algin chuckled, the sound warming Maira. It had been way too long since she heard that wind-chime laughter. "I gwine."

Maira gaped. "Really?"

"Why not? Least they wan wi dey."

Maira's arm itched, the skin tight with healing. She rubbed a drop of resinous oil into developing scar. "We can't live on Mars. We can't create a civilization."

Algin pursed her unpainted lips. "So? Looka what had happen wit Sanding."

The Sanding had launched for Mars with a crew of twelve of the finest minds of a generation, their voyage and arrival trending worldwide. Shock when the mission lost contact with Earth. Tragedy months later when contact was restored to find only one survivor: a thin, copper-skinned man, Dr. Bennett Brockington. Maira couldn't recall his line of study, only that he'd had so many letters after his name, the news decreased the font size to get his full credentials on the screen.

He only spoke five words: I am a witch. Travel.

I am a witch. Travel. On the first anniversary of his return to Earth, he died. Later, it was found Dr. Brockington wasn't a witch, but he'd studied several wondercraft rituals. He'd dabbled, he'd read, but he hadn't learned.

He wasn't practicing full.

Travel. Traveler. Welcome.

Maira bit her lip. "You sure about this?"

When Algin nodded, Maira rocked back on her heels. What the hell was happening? Algin was usually the voice of reason, her graceful hand grasping Maira's ankle to keep her grounded when she reached the end of her tether. What was she supposed to do when her rock defied gravity?

"T'ink on 'em." When Maira agreed, Algin let herself out.

Alone once again, she filled a clear bowl with water and stared at it—through it, searching, scrying—for hours until her back ached and her eyes were dry and pulsing, but she got no answers. Finally, she gave up. Rubbed her skin with lavender and oatmeal milk and went to sleep.

The next day, she woke to an email.

Wild ONe,

Will you come? Wwe wait for you. To come and bring others. Do not fear. No fear. Bring and come. Bring yourself wildone.

To our wilds space. Run. Here. B free.

The email wasn't signed and the sender's address didn't make sense. It was: WeLcomequorum*mrz.ms

Maira rubbed her eyes. They were tired, gritty with use, as though she'd been looking for something all night while she slept. She usually didn't watch TV in the mornings, preferring to get her news from trusted online sources. But today, she wanted to listen to what the world had to say.

All she heard was more babbling, confusion over the phenomena in the sky. It had been worldwide, reaching metropolis and village alike, but had only lasted a few seconds. No official government comment yet, but many were claiming it to be a hoax, an elaborate prank by some wacko sympathizer.

Maira wasn't sure if they meant a witch sympathizer or a Martian one, but she was sure it wasn't a prank. It hit too close to home, plucking a string in her heart. Her entire essence thrummed with power. Intent.

If it wasn't a prank, what was it? The unknown was her biggest fear. A known quantity, she could face, but this—she hesitated to use the word *opportunity*, but she couldn't come up with a better one—was the ultimate unknown. And how was she going to get there? Show up at a space station and say she was signing up to the spellcaster program? Or maybe a ship would descend from nowhere to enclose all witcheren and speed them to the red planet.

Ridiculous. But the melting indigo sky and that email, full of strange yet needful words that resonated inside her like the vibrations of a gong.

Wild one Wild one.

Welcome

Maybe it was time to go. To find new places where we all could be free.

Wild one . . .

Part of it was fear, and the rest of it was doubt, weighty and crippling. Questions swirled within her as well, breeding excuses for why she couldn't leave. Fear of success was still fear. Suppose those empty colonies couldn't hold them all? How could they get food? How could they live?

There were structures built. Seeds and silos of water. But that would be all. There was no way the Earth would supplement them once the witches left. We would be there all on our own.

B free.

"Are you ready?"

"Uh huh."

Maira noticed Algin had a duffle bag. She always traveled light, but realization dawned on her as though she were falling off a cliff—fast, breath-stealing.

"How we 'pose fuh do 'em?"

"I think . . ." she swallowed. "I think we got an invitation."

At Algin's raised eyebrow, Maira pulled up the email on her laptop, turned the screen. Algin mouthed the words, stoic face neutral. "You right, Tittuh."

Tittuh. Whenever Algin called her sister, it jolted her to a stop. Living close together, they'd had their share of arguments—some that ended because they'd agreed to disagree. Some because they promised to jump to the next topic, move away from damaging each other. Tittuh meant: I'm with you wholeheartedly on this. We are here. Together.

Maira nodded, hit reply. In the empty box, she typed:

"We are honored to accept your invitation. Please send instructions on how to reach you."

Algin approved the message with a shrug and a nod.

"Last chance to change your mind."

"Nuh uh." Algin swirled the ice in her glass and downed the rest of the drink in one gulp. Winced. "I tyed a dis."

Maira was tired of it too. She hit send.

Within moments, a response appeared:

Wild ONeS,

You are come. Do this. Do and Bring yourselfs wild oneS.

B free.

>>Blood of frozen

>Some Love

>A dreme

>Some pain

>>> Some Time

Wwe wait for you.

Again, there was no signature.

"Is that a list of . . . ingredients?"

"A hex?" Algin was intrigued. Maira could see the flicker of interest in her countenance, a reminder of when times were better, when she smiled more, laughed even. That hadn't been in a while.

"Looks like it. I think." Maira bit her lip. "But what are these ingredients— blood of frozen? Some pain?"

"You know you's always cold."

Algin's soft words rocked Maira back in her chair. She was frozen in more ways than one. Her life, iced into this routine of gathering food while being hunted. Her inability to connect to this world the way she wanted to—needed to—in order to be whole. Maira took the bloodied handkerchief out of her bag. It was crumpled, stiff, but that didn't matter. It was her blood, gone cold.

She didn't hear Algin get up, but her friend now stood at her shoulder, handing her a fist-sized cobalt blue bottle. When Maira looked up in askance, Algin spoke quietly, her body turned toward the moonlight-filled window.

"I cry sometime, missin' what we been, but I 'pose . . . I mos' skeert of what we gone be. Martyrs? Ghosts? Myths?" She shrugged her narrow shoulders, draped as they always were in a flowing hooded cape. "So . . . you got my pain. Summa it."

Algin's stare nudged her as effectively as an elbow, and Maira nodded at her tittuh. "Okay, let's cook."

In Maira's snug kitchen, they pored over the recipe Algin had jotted down on the back of a torn open envelope. Despite the warmer temperature, Maira reached for her shawl. Before she could drape it over her, Algin reached out and plucked the handkerchief from her fingers and dropped it into a glass jar.

Together, they completed the spell with the dream stones from under their pillows, a handful of the foraged berries they both loved, along with a sprinkling of the precious sugar. Maira gently placed the collar her Muffin used to wear on top. She'd found it the day the felines left, and she'd kept it in her cedar chest ever since. Before screwing on the lid, Algin poured in the contents of the bottle of pain.

"Now what do we do?"

Again Algin's elegant shrug.

"Let's go sit." Maira pushed the jar into a patch of moonlight and headed for the living room sofa. For what seemed like hours they talked, strong liquor coursing through them.

Maira woke, head fuzzy and eyes tacky. She groaned. Still in the house. Nothing had changed. When she looked at the clock above the mantelpiece, it showed the time as being near midnight.

"We're still here," she whispered to herself, in order to not wake Algin.

But Algin was already awake and straightening her cape. Somehow, her long, dark hair was still in place. "We muss up?"

"I don't know. The spell was confusing, so maybe. How do you feel?"

"My head ackin' up. Yours?"

Maira touched her temples with firm pressure. "A little lightheaded, yeah. But that's not anything. Could be the alcohol."

"Maybe issa joke." Algin touched her cheek with thoughtful fingers. "And we fools fuh believing."

"Wanting better is never foolish." She held her arms out, but remembered Algin didn't care for hugs. "Sorry, forgot."

"More glug?"

"Yeah, come on." Maira led the way back to the kitchen to make another round of drinks. Then they could turn in for the night. She hurried to mix and measure, keeping busy so the pain of her failure wouldn't show. But it rose in her, the sour taste of defeat. Hopefully, the drink would mask the flavor. A hand met her shoulder and she jumped.

"What— oh sweet Florida water."

Outside the kitchen window stretched a cloudless butterscotch sky. Mountains in the distance, but mostly an expanse of land as far as her eyes could see. They walked to the door. Maira put her hand out when Algin went to open it.

"No, we can't. Breathe. This is . . . impossible."

To her surprise, Algin placed a hand on Maira's shoulder. "We welcome, 'member?"

"How can you tell? I mean, we don't know if—" Her words stopped as she watched a fan of saw palmetto grow from the previously empty ground. It was a curious dusky pink instead of green, but there was no mistaking its shape. Another joined it, followed by a blue-fruited lemon tree and tightly-coiled patches of wild thyme.

"Oh," she said.

Algin opened the door so it didn't make a sound. While they looked on, another building appeared in the distance, and soon after, a gnarled, live oak tree reached its arms wide as if seeking an embrace.

"How . . . how can this be happening?"

"Mars is fuh witches," Algin said, grinning. She slipped a hand into Maira's and they set off across the expanse to greet their neighbors.

Graverobbing Negress Seeks Employment

I PRIED APART THE CORPSE'S LIPS, THEIR SLACKNESS TELLING ME SHE'D BEEN dead more than two days, and worked the tip of my finger inside her mouth. It opened enough for me to wedge the funnel in, its tip clinking on her teeth. I tipped my porcelain-lined hip flask—metal was a no-no—to spill the tea into her mouth. She didn't have to swallow; enough would make its way down for the magic to work. I leaned back from the shallow hole she lay in, my aged joints protesting something fierce, then recapped the hip flask before hiding it away with the funnel inside my stocking. Wasn't nobody looking up these skirts.

Tonight was kind. The temperature along Charleston Harbor had dropped, creating a soupy fog the moon couldn't quite cut through. Enough light to see my way home but too little to give busybodies a clear view. My ear was always open to the rustle of feet or the clop of hooves approaching, except I wouldn't have to worry about avoiding carriages tonight—those horses' eyes weren't good in the dark no way. Even so, I looked around me as I crouched on the pile of fresh turned dirt next to her, waiting.

She stirred. A brief jolt like she'd been run through with a tease of lightning. When her eyes opened—the first thing they all did was open their eyes—they were just starting to turn milky. I took her hand and helped her rise from the pit she'd been thrown in.

"Come on, honey. Maybe in your next life, you'll learn to pick better men."

Her dress was ripped, exposing one small breast; her hem was stained stiff with blood and fluids. Did the best I could with arranging the little coils of her hair to cover the angry rope burns around her neck and the hole in her skull, 'cause tea don't fix everything. I wrapped my cape around her narrow shoulders and leaned her back against a tree while I filled in the hole. Then we started walking: her with an awkward bow-legged hobble and me not much better.

Chilled wind blew in, clearing the dense blanket of fog, and I hurried our steps. A hurricane lantern burned in the back window of one of the little shotgun houses off Maple Street and we headed toward it, avoiding the backyards because of the dogs yowling, torn between the need to protect their territory and their fear of the dead. I tapped on the closed screened door with a ragtime rhythm, and after some scrabbling and heated whispers, it opened.

"Oh, thank you, Jesus." The woman inside, young-looking with old eyes, sagged against the uneven doorframe when she saw the pair of us. Her man stood behind, large and silent and watchful.

"You got a place for her to be?" I asked. The effect of the tea wouldn't last forever, and having a dead body lying around wasn't good for no one, especially not Colored folk.

"Baby?" the woman asked.

The girl turned toward the voice. "I'm so sorry, Mama." The words came out thickened and slow, pushed past the decaying tongue. The girl's mama broke down, sobs wrenching from her throat as she pulled and tore at the scarf covering her head.

Her man came to her, took the woman and her daughter each by an arm, and led them to a sturdy, homemade table. He set a kettle on the stove to boil, then slid my cape off the girl's shoulders, folded it, then returned it to me. As he pressed coins into my hand, he said, "Reb Fielding got a special little place for her to rest in the St. Matthew graveyard now that she home." His eyes skitted away from mine. "How long we got?"

I reared back to look at the sky. The moon hadn't reached its high point yet, still a ways to go before sunrise. "Til day clean. 'Round five or six hours."

"Thankee now."

I nodded and headed off home. Cold was creeping in on the evening, and I pulled my cape tighter. Time for my own cup of tea.

The sandy-haired Negro boy gave me the signal. Casual-like, I turned to notice the street cart where it sat with its hand-painted sign—P'nut Man & Hot Fried—and made my way over.

"How much for a lil bag?"

"Half penny, Miz Prosper." He shook his head slightly as he said it and I knew there was news. "Got some hot fried that's good today though."

"Please for some."

I watched as he dropped a scoopful of chicken gizzards coated with seasoned corn meal into the hot grease and set the lid back on the cast iron kettle. Sun was blessing the day with warm breeze, but the heat coming off the cart felt good in my bones. He sold a couple steaming bags of boiled peanuts to some longshoremen, who clomped away to put in their time loading and unloading the ships, leaving empty brown shells sucked dry of briny juice to litter the walkway. The boy fished my hot fried out, sprinkled them with salt, then placed the crispy bits in newspaper, folded real careful-like. I handed him five pennies, and he started to refuse, but I pressed them into palm. He looked at me with damp eyes and closed his fingers around the money, the back of his hand marked with scattered grease burns in circles and lines, a dark Morse Code on his light-brown skin.

"Keep that. If you get the chance, you look out for me, hear?"

"Yas'm. Thank you, ma'am."

I knew he already did, like most of the other Coloreds 'round here. If they didn't, I mighta been caught long ago. Even though most church-going Negroes claimed to be scared of me, saying what I did wasn't natural, I eased their minds by returning their kin to them so they could rest on blessed ground. Whispers about me had been going around the city for years, in the parlors and in the paper mills, on the farms and in the ironworks. If you can find your dead, then you better next find Miss Prosper.

Most of my work was from lynchings—Negroes dragged off to their ends for talking back, for having a business that started to cut into the white man's, or for having independence of mind. Sometimes an unwelcome suitor who after the fire of passion died, dug a shallow grave to hide his shame. Might think it gets easier over the years, but no.

Even though my customers welcomed their dead back, I could see their deeper thoughts—anybody messin' with life and death can't be right with God.

Of course, I ain't evil, but what most minds can't get a grip on . . . they call the devil's work. I don't work for Old Scratch, though I expect I'll meet him one day if talk makes things true.

I turned my attention to the paper as I walked away, popping a steaming hot gizzard in my mouth. The chewy meat split as I bit into it, letting a stream of rich juice coat my tongue. Searching for the line that spoke directly to me, I found the young man had kept it just out of reach of the grease splashes:

Employ Available—Negress Preferred
A remover for a large number of fragile items is promptly needed. On the main street of this city, a few doors down from the courthouse. The terms may be known by applying therein.

The word courthouse was run through with two lines, striking it out. Next to it, written in lead pencil, was the word *blacksmith's*. After reading, I rolled the rest of the chicken onto the marked paper, letting the grease cover up the pencil marks. Then I finished my lunch and headed home to make the Life Everlasting.

Big Mama taught me how to make the Life Everlasting when I was a girl. It was from a recipe brought over here from Senegal, or somewheres. Like their jollof rice became our red rice, the recipe changed from family to family until nobody really knew which one was the first. I'd heard her and my gran, both strong root ladies, talking about it when they was making other teas to keep away fellas the ladies didn't want, to keep bosses sweet, to win at the numbers . . . But I'd had to prove myself time and time again before they would teach me this blend.

"Never use this 'less you have to, hear?" Big Mama told me before she lay out all what went in the tea. "Little glug, Prosper . . . Only little glugs 'til you's sure how much to take. And make it weak at first."

I still lay out the ingredients for the tea like she taught me that first day so long ago. What was it? Ninety years or so now? I wondered what they would think of me using their tea to move the dead. Shoot, maybe they already knew what I used it for.

It was getting harder to find everything now, but I found I could make small changes and have the tea work just fine. Long as I could get pepper berry and sun gold root, it'd be okay. The redbush tea leaves and kola nuts I grew myself.

I steeped everything in my clay pot, no metal could touch this blend, then left it to cool. Once I strained it through two layers of muslin, it would be ready. I stoked the flames in my fireplace to warm the room and keep my hands from shaking. I had to fill the jars careful-like, not wanting to waste a drop of my hard work.

A knock came on my door, gentle like it was scared, but firm like it had run outta choice. If they stood at my door, they likely had.

I opened the door to see a wide-eyed boy, not more than eight or ten, on the step. He was breathing hard, musta been running like a bat outta torment. His high-water pants with no socks told me all I needed to know.

"Come on in here now, chile."

He was scared, and I couldn't blame him. No idea what kinda stories he heard about me. But I knew what I looked like, right 'round forty or fifty some odd years old—old enough to command like a wise woman but spry enough to do the job. When the cold got in these bones though, I felt every one a my hundred years. I never was pretty, but that was a blessing my mother had given me. Pretty women caught too many eyes. And hands.

The boy edged inside, keeping his hand on the doorknob. His eyes darted around like flies on roadkill.

"You want something to eat? Drink?" He shook his head roughly. "Didn't think so. Well, why you here? Crack ya teeth, son."

"They foun' my brother."

"Who chile is you?"

"Francis Station, ma'am."

I whistled long and low. Francis Station's son had been missing for years, since Mayor Bradley found out his daughter had been sniffing around him. I can't say he wasn't sniffin' too, but he shoulda known not to let nobody see them together. Heard some white man dragged him from behind one of them machines he used to work on at the paper mill and nobody seen him since.

"Where?" I asked.

"Out the marsh by Runnin' Jack place. 'Neath that sick-looking poplar tree. I made a mark like they said I was to."

I sat back in my chair. Dangerous. Jack ran numbers and liquor, but he wouldn't stand for nobody on his property. I don't know how the boy got out there and back 'cause Jack tended to shoot first and never ask questions. They say not to trust crackers who live near Negroes. I had to hope I could get in and outta there quick and not let him catch me.

"All right, chile." The job in the paper had to wait. Had to hope they'd understand. "I'll go, but—"

The boy held out his hand, stopping my words. Two Stella coins lay in his palm. "Mama said she know it ain't safe, so she'll pay you first. And two more when you get him."

Sixteen dollars total. Christ rising. I took the coins and patted the boy on the shoulder. "You tell her I'mma go there tonight."

"Yes'm."

After he left, I sat there for about an hour, looking at the door until nightfall, the moon and stars lighting up my table. Then I filled my flask, tied the funnel to its neck, got my shovel, and left the house. The tea was still warm where it pressed against my inside thigh. I'd had a swig of it myself earlier, and it erased the ache in my joints, gave me a bit more energy. The shovel I tied to the inside of my cape, and it bounced silently against my generous bottom as I walked to where the marshland met the dirt.

Outta the corner of my eye, I could see Runnin' Jack's place edged up against the marsh, where fireflies dove in and around the reeds. Big ol' house but not much to look at with its peeling paint and flaking wood. Barn didn't look much better. Splintered wheels and broken buggies dotted the backyard. All was quiet save for the chorus of frog song, making me think this was just gonna be like any other cemetery visit.

Sorry to say it wasn't.

I managed to find the poplar tree with its white chalk mark slash pretty easy. It was sick, likely from the rot in the soul of the person who buried the dead here. I loosened my shovel from inside my cape and said a swift prayer that this was gonna be a cakewalk.

A patch of grass lifted away in one straight piece. Underneath, a layer of earth was loose, releasing the smell of rich soil. I scraped it away. Against the black dirt, white bone shined. The boy must have stopped here and run to his mama because the rest of the dig was into harder dirt, like the earth had to make up for the soft, dank pluff mud of the marsh just feet away. Glad I didn't have to come through that way. Charleston was famous for its pluff mud, and even binyahs like me lost a shoe once or twice to its sucking hold.

I grunted as the shovel only broke through fingernail-sized bits of dirt at a time, making me use elbow grease I didn't have. Hot and sweaty, I stopped for a moment, easing my back upright, taking big glugs of the cool air off the marsh.

It held the sweetness of life and death, swampy and ocean cool. I lost myself in it and didn't hear the footsteps approaching.

He tackled me from behind, holding my legs together, and sent me headfirst toward the base of the tree where it poked through the hard-pack dirt. I kept from slamming my face into the gnarled roots of the poplar by twisting my body and taking the knock on my shoulder. The wind flew out of me, and I rolled to my back, the shovel thudding to the ground. I heard Jack grab for it and toss it away. His weight felt like a stone where he had me pinned to the ground, pressing his man parts against me like we played night games. His face was weathered, pale skin drawn tight against his skull. Salt and pepper whiskers and a beat-up fishing hat covered most of what else I tried to see. But those rabbit-gray eyes held me sure as his body.

"What're you doing on my land?" He growled the question out, and its scent reached me, swimming in tobacco and fish grease. He fumbled for something in his pants, and my breath caught, but he just pulled out a revolving gun, the kind Army men tended to have. Satisfied I had seen it, he lay it against my belly.

There was something in his face that I knew. I couldn't place it, but it was there. The shape of his brow, the line of grizzled hair running along his cheek? I saw it, felt it in my spirit. Knew it as sure as I could breathe. Breeze blew up off the marsh, shifting the clouds and letting more of the moon's smile through to touch his pale face so close to mine. The answer called to me in a memory of blood.

"You a Negro," I whispered.

"And you're a witch. Facts neither one of us wants told." He cocked the gun. "Now where's that leave us, Miss Prosper?"

I eyed the oiled-metal barrel, then frowned. "With you lettin' me sit up off this cold ground."

He thought about it, then sat back, freeing my legs. I shuffled to sit up, smoothing my long skirt down. He didn't help, just watched me with them rabbit-fur-gray eyes and tapped the gun on his knee.

"Why're you here?" he asked again.

"To do a job. You got a child buried out here, Mr. Jack and I—"

"You ain't taking nothing from my property."

"What? I'm talking about a child. His mama just want to bury him. That's all."

He shook his head.

"A boy someone lynched for looking sideways at a girl, that's all. A Negro boy. Or don't you care about your own people?"

His eyes stayed on mine, and I shivered like ghosts was looking in my face. "I said you are not to take a thing off my property."

Frustrated, I thumped the ground with my fists. I had nothing, no weapon, and I felt foolish for never thinking to bring one. Never needed to before. "It's a dead, Jack, a dead! Why you wanna keep a dead here?"

He thought about my question, then he spat out a thick wad of wet tobacco. "Leave 'em be. No good comes of draggin' up the past."

As he sat on the cold ground looking down at me, I realized. Whispers said it was white men who had taken them children off over the years to God only knew what kinda fate. And it never occurred to me that someone might use that fact to hide his own sins.

Real fear took me then, and I shook with it. "It was you. All this time." When he didn't say anything, I yelled. "Wasn't it?"

"Whites kill coloreds all the time." Jack worked a finger into his ear, digging. Wiped it clean on his dungarees. "Everybody knows that. I just had to make sure I picked the right ones; ones they woulda gotten to eventually. All I had to do was keep to myself and dig fast."

I felt tears burn my eyes, run down my face in hot trails. "Why?" I choked on the word. The marsh grass *shooshed* in the still air.

He shrugged. "I can't help killin'. I need it . . . like breathing."

My heart flipped in my chest. I searched the ground for something, anything, to use to save my life. The tea running through my system would buy some time, but it wouldn't heal me from gunshot. A flicker caught my eye, and I saw the cutting edge of the shovel for a moment as the clouds passed over. Nestled against the marsh reeds, out of reach.

Jack got to his feet, towering over where I sat on the ground next to the half-dug hole. He'd probably finish digging it and slide me in next to the dead.

"It keeps me calm. Helps me sleep." Training the gun on me, he turned up first one shirt sleeve, then the other. "I plan to sleep well tonight."

"You sho is, Mister Jack." The voice came from behind him and as he spun around, the crack of a rifle followed.

His head flung back like he was about to offer up a prayer, but I knew that couldn't be as I could see the sky through his skull. He swayed, crashed to the ground. Slow-like, his body fell back, meeting up with the trunk of the poplar.

I swung my head to see Francis Station lowering her husband's rifle, and my breath eased out of me. Her young boy, the one who had come to me earlier, stood behind her. They were both barefoot, feet covered in shiny-brown pluff mud from the marsh up to the ankles.

"My boy told me you was coming tonight. I just . . . wanted to see."

I didn't ask why she thought she had to bring a gun, but I was grateful, and I told her so. "Glad you came, honey. I 'preciate you."

We both dug, me with the shovel and her with the hoe that the boy had brought along. Soon, we uncovered what was left of a reed-thin young man, once handsome from the way his bones and what was left of his dark skin came together. I tried to cover most of the rot with my cape, but she stopped me.

"No, I wanna see him. His pa . . . ain't gone want to."

"Alrighty." No need to pull away the lips; they were mostly gone. I poured the tea through the exposed teeth, where it ran across and down into the space just before the jawbone hinged to the rest of the skull.

While we waited, she asked, "Can you make him whole? Just for a little while? It's been"—she cleared her throat—"a long time."

"No, I can't," I said, grateful that tea can't fix everything. I didn't want *that* magic. "Spend this little time you have with him, then let him rest. That's always my advice."

She pressed her lips together but nodded, and I was sure she'd heed me. I turned to the rustling now coming from the makeshift grave. "Come on now. Time for you to get on home."

I parted with the Station family at the top of their road, promising to show up at the services if I was able. I guzzled the rest of the Life Everlasting I'd made on my way home, hoping it would ease my aches and bruises. As I shuffled along, I was starting to wonder if I was up to whatever the job for the blacksmith was. How was I supposed to remove any more fragile items when I felt like one myself?

I chafed my fingers, the brief warmth fighting off the creeping chill of the hushed night. And how many was a "large number," anyways? Ten? Twenty? Sure, I could brew up enough tea, but what about the cost to myself? Seeing my people broken up and beat down, tore and tattered, made me weary. Forever after, I'd be wondering how many of 'em Jack killed after giving in to that mad fever in his head. A few more empty streets brought me shuffling up to my doorstep. Never have I been so happy to see my little house, but it made my mind run on how many others was out there waiting to be found, so they could catch they final little piece a home.

Once inside, I made myself a cup of Forty Winks tea to help me sleep. Something to calm my mind, help me stop thinking about this last job, what it meant to my peace and my future in this town. I breathed in the scent of magnolia bark and mulungu and took a small sip. I shook myself at the taste— like perfume on dry roots—and said a silent prayer for God to guide my mind. All the while knowing I was gonna take that job, no matter how dangerous it was. I stayed up all night, drinking that brew and staring out into the dark, because tea don't fix everything.

The Salt Cure

Monday—

I AM NOT HUNGRY, BUT I PLACE SALT FLAKES ON MY TONGUE, ALLOW THE hard edges to melt into a briny liquor. I eat olives, anchovies, Parma ham, shake soy into my mouth, follow it with strips of bacon.

It has been raining for days, and outside, the ground is saturated with water, running in rivulets through my garden, over the carefully laid stone path that winds and wavers in an attempt to lure the monsters and the demons away from my door.

Most times it works. But lately, they have been coming closer and closer—I can hear their howls, the scratch-scritch of their claws. One got almost to the roof, and I could hear its feet scuttling on the mortar, but my wards held.

When it is dry, I surround my house and garden with coarse salt and ground red brick to protect it—and me. But with this torrential rain, the salt and brick wash away, leaving the house vulnerable.

I have no control over the elements; I cannot stop the deluge of savagery saturating this last stronghold of peace. And so I have no choice but to make myself the protection.

In my mortar I grind salt with oil, add pimento. Spread it on my tongue like a paste. The sharpness makes me shudder and my nipples harden.

Outside, the rain drives and the demons rustle, preparing for battle.

I am not ready yet. But I will be.

Tuesday—

Salted cashews are creamy, almost milky in my mouth, and I suck on them like teats before crushing them on my back teeth. Follow them with crab roe that crunches like good crystal under a boot heel and cornichons tart enough to make me wince.

I try not to exert myself too much—I don't want to sweat away the salt filling my body.

Am I a sacrifice?

I'll know soon.

Wednesday—

My tongue feels rough, almost shriveled; I say grace before I eat again and ask for blessings from my ancestors. My grandmother's spirit has always given me her guidance, but she has instructed me to fight my own battles. I wonder if she will intervene this time to stop the monsters threatening my door—the door that separates this world from the next.

Skittering and gleeful chitter tells me they slink ever closer.

The house grows hot, then the heat ebbs to cool, descends to frost. I question my strength. No, the voice inside me—the one that recalls my stumbles, my fear, my indecision—asks: *Who do you think you are? You can't win. You can't destroy them all. You are but one.*

I warm bouillon on the cast-iron stove, add drops of lemon juice, then drink it down, the dried vegetables scraping my raw throat.

Is this what it takes to become protection? Is this what it takes to become a god? No, I will never be a god. A priestess, perhaps. A lowly kitchen witch taking on the fight of the ages. Whatever I am, I am the last.

But can I take this punishment? I am but one.

A hiss comes from outside, I turn to see a shadow dart away from my window. So it begins.

I rush over to close the curtains, but I decide against it. Best that I am able to see them when they come. Look the end in the face. If I survive this battle, it will be a miracle.

Cheese from cow, ewe, and goat—all tangy, salty savor. The door rattles on its hinges, and rainwater leeches in under a crack in the frame, running in rivulets toward my bare feet.

Their numbers double, triple. They have brought the rains to sweep me away, so they can roam this world free. Free to devour those that only seek to live their lives away from pain and torment. From the weight of judgment that will always find them lacking.

Sleep does not come, nor do I wish it to.

Thursday—

I greet the day with red eyes that see clearly. My body shakes. Across the garden, through the rain, they come. Their steps judder and jump. Some crawl, but most are standing upright, confident of victory.

I can see their teeth, white fangs bright under the gray rainy skies. Howls of pleasure, or anticipation, reach me, and I bare my own fangs.

Let them come.

I get my wish. They rush forward in droves, rain sluicing off their hides, their footfalls pounding the earth. My door rattles as I open it, face my fate. The first one dissolves at the touch of my finger. Unable to stop their rampage, dozens more shatter when they collide with me. Others dissolve, their screams hellish and comforting.

Confused, some hang back. Why isn't she afraid? Why doesn't she run? They hesitate, waiting to see the outcome . . . hoping there will be something left to pick clean.

Not these bones.

Let them taste of me. Let my blood salt this earth, soaking into the soil to nourish the grasses that will then shoot up, twisting and twining, tying the monsters up, trapping them in a prison of their own making. Do not come for me, or you will be sent back to whatever hell you left.

A seizure takes me. I shake as though someone is trying to wake me from a dream. No. Not now.

Their howls of triumph erupt, grow louder.

I squeeze my eyes shut, run forward into the rain. My skin slicks as it dissolves and I fling my arms wide, releasing swirls of opaque salinized slush that strikes the monsters like burning whips. They scream, almost as loud as I do while I flail. All that I have prepared, all that I have become, turning to sludge.

The monsters circle me, but they are wary. Afraid once again. They see the sacrifice I am willing to make and it makes them cowardly, unsure of their power in the face of a kitchen priestess god at the end of her tether.

I rage, saline and brick and my own blood now strewn around the garden. More of them suffer though, as I watch—almost unseeing—in the storm. The howls fade, growing distant.

It is a good thing, because I am also fading. Sinking into the soil, now drenched and mucky. I close my eyes slowly, then open them, knowing I have given my all, my everything, and it is now time to stop. My feet have sunk into the dirt and I try to pull them out, but I see they have partially dissolved into the earth. My hands have eroded too. I tumble to the ground, pull myself toward the house, arm over arm, toward the open door. I manage to get inside, place my worn shoulder against the frame and push it closed.

Rest.

I close my eyes again.

Whispers cover me. Hands, butterfly light, work on my wounds. A floral, ethereal scent wafts from them, like the fragrance of the gardenia I place on grandmother's grave every year. Only now I realize how much I hurt, inside and out, but mostly, I am shaken. Monsters still call in the failing darkness, but the sounds are far away, and growing fainter. I open my eyes.

The rain has stopped and the growing sunlight is almost blinding, but I can see their shadows. Their hands redraw my wards, crush fresh brick with salt, feed me soup—a meaty brine that begins to restore me to myself.

I thought I was alone. The last.

My mouth is dry and the words are a struggle.

Jewelry jangles from necks and ears and wrists while they work, leaving the sound of change in the air.

Never for long, they reply.

For Southern Girls
when the Zodiac
Ain't Near Enough

T HE WOMAN YOU GO TO SEE FOR YOUR READING ISN'T OLD, BUT HER eyes have aged more than her skin as if she's seen horrors but hasn't learned to hide them. Her name online is Butter, and you see why. She's a punkinskin, her complexion high yellow and dotted with freckles. Long braids adorned with brass clasps brush her forearms as she gestures for you to take the seat across from her with a hand adorned with silver rings.

As you sit on the chair, a huff of air releases from the embroidered cushion, scented with dogwood blossom and dried sweetgrass, mixing with your nervous sweat. At the door, she asked you to remove your shoes, and after a moment of hesitation, you did, and now your bare toes curl uselessly against the jute rug.

Butter offers you a drink, but you refuse. Your mama taught you not to drink from everybody. She isn't offended, or doesn't seem to be. Instead, she settles into an overstuffed chair, then folds her right leg underneath herself. When she pulls her left leg up, a chain of shiny dimes around her ankle jingles like a wind chime heralding a storm. She tugs her long skirt down and looks at you expectantly.

"I want to know my future."

You don't say, *I feel lost.* You don't say, *It's all too much.* Life—just living—is so hard, and I'm tired of the hate and the hurt. You smooth the fabric of your good jacket, the one you save for funerals. It's been getting too much wear lately.

"My sign is—"

She holds up a hand. "Where you from?" she asks, and you tell her.

"Hmm, a Southern gal. I don't need your star sign. The ones you know are not for us." Her accent is languid and loose, the song of the South, of lazy days and sticky nights, and her words creep closer on tiny legs to whisper in your ear. "They don't tell the whole story of how we are."

She pulls a deck of cards from the drawer of a walnut-hued buffet table. They're almost larger than her hands, but she grips their worn softness firmly and with confidence. On the backs of the cards is a batik print, blue and white, bleeding into flowers.

"You can learn, grow, run all you want. But the South never leaves you. Its aches and pains are yours, but its future may not be."

She shuffles the deck, the sound a fleeting ruffle. "Shall we see?"

You wait heartbeats before realizing her question wasn't rhetorical. You nod.

"I'll place these cards here on the dining table in the zodiac spread, a circle of twelve running counterclockwise." She places the deck in front of you on the wooden tabletop crisscrossed with nicks and scars. "Now cut."

Without a thought, you reach out, lift off more than half the deck, and place it next to the shorter stack. Butter takes the shorter stack and places it on top of the larger, then flips the top card and places it on the table with a snap.

Rice:

The card shows not a bowl of rice, but the plant itself, green stalks bent forward under the weight of beige-husked grain.

A voice speaks, melodious and silvery, yet resonant enough to echo within your mind and heart. Your gaze flips to Butter, but while her lips are parted, they don't move. Her head is tilted to one side as though she's listening along with you.

People born under the sign of this revered food understand creativity, even though they may not trust their own. They know the origins of things. That what many know as truth about your people is not so. Until the lion has its historian, all tales of the hunt will celebrate the hunter.

Centuries have been spent separating you from what you were meant to be. You will have to spend many hours, perhaps your lifetime, learning to put yourself back together.

Butter flips the next card, placing it down and to the right of the first.

Oak Tree:

Self-sufficiency is your mantra.

You are like the largest oak in the South—the Boar Hog Tree. It stood for many years alone, growing of its own accord until the day the city came to cut it down. It reached out then, calling for help—too late for its people to save it.

"You're strong and capable but don't know when to ask for help." The sound of Butter's actual voice after the unearthly one is a shock, but you manage not to jump. Her eyes don't waver when she says, "This'll kill you. If you let it."

The third card parts the curtain of silence that fell at her words.

Cast Iron:

Testify.

You have seen much and endured more. You feel the pain of those around you, but don't know how to help. You have no idea that just a few scrapings of yourself are enough to heal.

Food prepared in cast iron becomes infused with the iron itself, easing the weakness of blood loss. Share your food, your words, that which you have made with the world and see how it soothes, invigorates others. Share, but remember to care for yourself.

Better yet, teach someone who wants to learn how to care for you.

Your eyes sting with unshed tears, and Butter must know the reading is true. Perhaps she knew before. This time, when she offers a drink, you accept.

While she is gone from the table, the desire to look at all the cards in the deck surfaces. Hearing your existence from another is deep, revealing, and you feel flayed open for the world to see. Why did you ask for this?

Maybe this reading of your soul can end quickly. But your hand shakes and you can't bring yourself to touch the cards. Your reader returns with a sweating glass; you take it without a tremble and drink. Sip after sip until you feel able to continue.

Snap.

The Marsh:

The picture is of the marsh at sunset, waning rays of light turning the tips of cattails to indigo and the water to honey-fire.

You draw people as there is something inside you that calls to others.

You embrace those kind to you, giving succor and solace. Your enemies are also lured in, but they meet a different fate—becoming mired in their jealousy, unable to extract themselves without great effort. Do not help them.

Marsh girls put off decisions, preferring to recall better, easier times.

"You got spirit music," Butter says. "That's what the old folk used to call it. Careful, though," she warns, "or you'll stagnate. Even marshes need a fresh supply of water to survive."

A drop of water from your glass falls to the tabletop, sinks into the wood, enriching its color.

Stop your drought.

The Front Porch:

The porch drawn on this card looks exactly like the one in front of the house you grew up in. But that . . . can't be. Upon closer inspection, you realize it is different, only just.

The people . . . oh, the people marching through your life are endless. Do they mean anything? Anything at all?

You encounter so many—on the street, at the gas station, on the train, at work, online. You barely look at them, only a rare glance when you feel brave. Rarer still, a person looks back. Gives a nod that means, *I see you, Sis.*

Yes, sometimes they mean everything. Let those that matter come and sit awhile.

June Bug:

You have no time to ponder this image as the voice begins to speak its evocative words before the card reaches the table.

Once, you were a free thing, crawling upon the trees, the dirt. Flying when you chose, which wasn't often.

Then you were caught. A string tied under your iridescent wings. Now when you fly, it's only a short distance, and in never-ending circles. But you remember your freedom, not at the end of a cord as some child's plaything.

When the child goes inside to eat or sleep, you chew through the string, releasing yourself back into the world. But a piece of that string remains, caught under your carapace, and it rubs . . . just enough to remind you of your brief captivity, and it spurs you on, crawling when you must but flying much more often now.

Your back aches. Right under the shoulder blades, and you press your shoulders down until there is a series of bubble-wrap pops. You feel something . . .

A string. It takes a while before you realize it's attached to your shirt and not to you.

Turtle:

The ancient wisdom of ancestors trudges through your life, giving the benefit of its long years. Serene, it edges forward, persevering through ridicule and jeering, through self-doubt and detractors. One step at a time.

A virtue, yes. But when you are able to move quickly, perhaps with a swift tide, do not be a fool and continue to plod.

"Want me to keep on, or do you need a break?"

Butter slips a small square into her mouth—a cracker, maybe. It crunches softly as if from a distance. You take one from the woven basket she proffers and place it on your tongue like a sacrament. Salt floods your mouth, and you're in the ocean. Its embrace is warm.

You ask her to go on, and the next card flicks from deck to table.

Okra:

Again, the picture on the card is of the plant, verdant green. You've never seen okra before it was picked, so you had no idea the pods grew upwards, away from the soil, defying gravity.

You aren't for everyone. Lots of people will hate you. You have an uncanny knack for having no idea of your effect on others. You might be tempted to change, be more conventional, but do not give in to this. There will be those that love you, but they will be few.

That is what you must accept: While others will have many, you will have few.

The urge to weep wells up inside you, and you manage to strangle it back. So few, too few . . .

Butter's eyes move back and forth over you, as though words are written on your skin. "You will have few," she repeats. "This is what you must accept."

You gulp down air to help you swallow this painful truth.

She takes the facedown deck and fans all the cards out, indicating you should choose three.

Cicada:

The insect is perched delicately on a camellia bud, its wings iridescent as cellophane. On the underside of the branch is a dried husk, curled in on itself. The cicada gazes, not at its former shell but off into the distance.

You've never liked bugs, and you frown.

"Don't give me that look," Butter says. "They're complex creatures, and people don't understand these symbols of immortality, rebirth."

Alone, you face danger, threats to your life and livelihood. When you band together with like minds, like hearts, you are able to overwhelm your predators. Lives may still be lost, yes, but most survive.

Find your sisters, keep them within reach of your song.

Collard:

Butter laughs, gently. "Shoulda known you'd pull this card."

People of this sign are born with strength in their cores: a toughness. Soon, more quickly than expected, frost touches your leaves. The frost of experience, of wisdom, of acceptance. It doesn't soften you completely, but it makes you aware of your own limitations.

You come from a place where the lapping waters are the color of collard-green liquor, and you wonder how many people met their first frost here. Your gran said to never pick collards that hadn't had frost lick their leaves. Maybe that applies to people too.

Then your thoughts turn to Butter, this young-old woman reading your life and arrowing your truth back into your heart. Does she have a family? Did she hone her gift under the watchful eye of her own grandmother?

You've convinced yourself to ask, but she turns over another card first. It surprises her.

And you.

Cotton:

"More pain," you whisper.

"Not necessarily." She runs her tongue over almost-straight, almost-white teeth.

In these cards, Cotton doesn't mean death, per se; it means change or the end of a difficult journey for a Cotton girl. This change doesn't come without memory. The slave ship is always in our blood, swaying. We move forward, recognizing the past as water we must wade in for a time. Children of the South, do not succumb. The shore is in sight.

"Final one," Butter says, plucking a card from the deck. She places it on the table, completing the circle.

You hold your breath.

The Haint:

The haint is shadowy one moment, distinct the next. A ghostly form shifting in and out of a background of Spanish-moss-draped fig trees. Its hands are cupped, holding something out to you, but you can't tell what.

Your future is there to grasp. Don't fear what holds it. There are many obstacles in life, which you could fall down on, and just as many places where you can step up. Trust your intuition, heed the message in every sign, each is within you. You are made of all the stars.

Rise.

The voice ebbs away, and the two of you sit in the quiet, absorbing, until Butter gathers the face-up cards, adding them to the rest of the deck. Shuffles with a soothing shoosh.

Your reading is over. While you want to process what has happened, your need to fill the quiet is overwhelming. Once you realize you don't know what to say, you stand up and head for the door. You've already paid online; what else is there to do?

After sitting for so long—how long isn't clear, but you can hear night song encroaching on your fellowship—your legs wobble. You're working your feet back into shoes when you remember your manners.

"Thank you for . . . well, thanks."

Butter lights a candle against the coming dark. The orange flame sparks, and for a moment, you see the shadow of something—someone—within her. Someone familiar and you smile. For the first time in a long while.

"Thank *you*," she replies, shyly returning your smile.

You know why she gave her thanks. For trusting her sight, for trusting the cards and the signs themselves.

As you head to your car, your stride is strong with intention. Purposeful. You look up into the sky. It is not quite dark, but the stars are emerging.

You are among them.

Publication History

"Every Good-Bye Ain't Gone" copyright 2018, first appeared in *Strange Horizons* 30 July 2018

"Sweetgrass Blood" copyright 2017, first appeared in *Sycorax's Daughters* (Cedar Grove Publishing)

"Folk" copyright 2017, first appeared in *Spook Lights II*

"A Cure for Ghosts" copyright 2017, first appeared in *Fireside*

"The Stringer of Wiltsburg Farm" copyright 2019, first appeared in *Vastarien: A Literary Journal* vol. 2, no. 2

"She Shells" copyright 2019, first appeared in the anthology *Gorgon: Stories of Emergence* (Pantheon Magazine)

"Room and Board Included, Demonology Extra" copyright 2021, first appeared in *Cooties Shot Required* (Broken Eye Books)

"Crickets Sing for Naomi" copyright 2017, first appeared in *PodCastle* 477

"How it Feels on the Tongue" copyright 2014, first appeared in *Up, Do: Flash Fiction by Women Writers* (Spider Road Press)

"Hands Made for Weaving, With Nails Like Claws" copyright 2019, first appeared in *Fireside*

"Shine, Blackberry Wine" copyright 2017, first appeared in *Shadows Over Main Street, Vol. 2* (Cutting Block Books)

Acknowledgements

THERE'S SO MUCH THAT GOES INTO PUTTING TOGETHER A COLLECTION. I'd like to thank those who assisted me in aligning the stars to bring *Who Lost, I Found* to fruition. While I'm sure I will accidentally leave out someone, please know it was not an intentional snub, just an oversight from an exhausted writer trying to remember with her sieve of a brain.

First, to my family for giving me the start in life they did, one full of stories and love for the written and spoken word. For sharing and singing and cooking and having open hearts and minds. For letting me disappear into books whenever I wanted and knowing that I'd be just fine.

To my wonderful husband for being you. Always.

To my fellow critique group writers, who were the first people who read some of these stories—in their earliest forms. Your feedback and support have been invaluable. While we no longer meet, I love and miss the time we spent together, reading each other's work and sharing our journeys. Hope to see all of you again, and I wish you successful, lasting careers.

To the editors who originally published these stories, thank you for amplifying my work.

To the authors of the books I've read for research and for my own enjoyment, which are too many to name. Thank you for sharing your worlds with me.

To those readers who love, purchase, share, recommend, shout about, feel seen by my work, you have my infinite thanks.

ƨ

Eden Royce is a writer from Charleston, SC. She's a Shirley Jackson Award finalist and has written articles for Writer's Digest and We Need Diverse Books. Her short fiction has appeared in a variety of print and online publications. Her debut novel *Root Magic* is a Walter Dean Myers Award Honoree, a Nebula Award finalist, and a Mythopoeic Fantasy Award winner for outstanding children's literature. Find her online at edenroyce.com.

BROKEN EYE BOOKS

Sign up for our newsletter at
www.brokeneyebooks.com

Welcome to Broken Eye Books! Our goal is to bring you the weird and funky that you just can't get anywhere else. We want to create books that blend genres and break expectations. We want stories with fascinating characters and forward-thinking ideas. We want to keep exploring and celebrating the joy of storytelling.

If you want to help us and all the authors and artists that are part of our projects, please leave a review for this book! Every single review will help this title get noticed by someone who might not have seen it otherwise.

And stay tuned because we've got more coming . . .

OUR BOOKS

The Hole Behind Midnight, by Clinton J. Boomer
Crooked, by Richard Pett
Scourge of the Realm, by Erik Scott de Bie
Izanami's Choice, by Adam Heine
Pretty Marys All in a Row, by Gwendolyn Kiste
The Great Faerie Strike, by Spencer Ellsworth
Catfish Lullaby, by A.C. Wise
Busted Synapses, by Erica L. Satifka
Boneset & Feathers, by Gwendolyn Kiste
Alphabet of Lightning, by Edward Morris
The Obsecration, by Matthew M. Bartlett

COLLECTIONS
Royden Poole's Field Guide to the 25th Hour, by Clinton J. Boomer
Team Murderhobo: Assemble, by Clinton J. Boomer
Who Lost, I Found: Stories, by Eden Royce

ANTHOLOGIES
(edited by Scott Gable & C. Dombrowski)
By Faerie Light: Tales of the Fair Folk
Ghost in the Cogs: Steam-Powered Ghost Stories
Tomorrow's Cthulhu: Stories at the Dawn of Posthumanity
Ride the Star Wind: Cthulhu, Space Opera, and the Cosmic Weird
Welcome to Miskatonic University: Fantastically Weird Tales of Campus Life
It Came from Miskatonic University: Weirdly Fantastical Tales of Campus Life
Nowhereville: Weird Is Other People
Cooties Shot Required: There Are Things You Must Know
Whether Change: The Revolution Will Be Weird

Stay weird.
Read books.
Repeat.

brokeneyebooks.com
twitter.com/brokeneyebooks
facebook.com/brokeneyebooks
instagram.com/brokeneyebooks

Printed in the USA
CPSIA information can be obtained
at www.ICGtesting.com
LVHW040804060923
757193LV00006B/123